GEMSTONES

THINGS TO BE GRATEFUL FOR & THINGS THAT ARE MISSED

IRENE MELLOTT

Reviewer: Jill Coutts

WESTBOW
P R E S S®
A DIVISION OF THOMAS NELSON
& ZONDERVAN

WestBow Press books may be ordered through booksellers or by contacting:

WestBow Press
A Division of Thomas Nelson & Zondervan
1663 Liberty Drive
Bloomington, IN 47403
www.westbowpress.com
844-714-3454

ISBN: 978-1-6642-3252-5 (sc)
ISBN: 978-1-6642-3251-8 (e)

Print information available on the last page.

WestBow Press rev. date: 11/02/2021

DEDICATION

To the women in my small group bible study:

Florence Tupper	Vicki Kern	Diane Carriere
Darleen Ferguson	Donna Mae Lambert	Linda Gellert
Marla Breitkreutz	Crystal Parrell	Jacqueline Snickerson
Tracy Madden	Stephine Borle	

Together we've shared biblical learnings and life experiences.
Thank you for your encouragement and
prayers. You've been a blessing to me.

CONTENTS

Things To Be Grateful For

Things That Are Missed

THINGS TO BE GRATEFUL FOR

CHAPTER 1

Casey stomped on her shovel with her work boot, overturning another mound of dirt. "Of all the open spaces surrounding our home, why did you decide to pick this particular spot, Dad? This patch must have the largest deposits of rocks on our property!"

Her father leaned against his shovel, wiping his brow with his shirtsleeve. "Because I've always wanted a rose garden, and this is the perfect place."

"No," she parried. "Perfect would have been by the house where cultivated gardens already exist."

"Is the work too hard for you?" he teased.

"As if! But, when you offered me a break from my studying, I didn't realize I'd be swapping mental work for physical labour."

Jeffrey chuckled at his eighteen-year-old daughter. "Perhaps you should have asked."

"I overheard you tell Jason that you had to pick up supplies. I assumed that meant we'd be driving into town," she said as she dug around the sides of a rock with her shovel until it had been worked free. Clutching it with both hands, she lifted it into the wheelbarrow, where it crash-landed on top of the others.

"Always check your assumptions," Jeffrey breathlessly replied as he staggered under the weight of the stone he carried to the trailer. A resounding thud soon followed. "Your brother had offered to pick up the fuel pump needed to repair the excavator. I told him I'd be picking it up as I had some errands to run. The part you missed was when I'd be going into town - tomorrow."

"Tomorrow!" she exclaimed, having thrown down her shovel. "Then why the manual labour? Once Old Digger is operational, it can find and dislodge these rocks so much quicker."

"The mini excavator may be small compared to our other farm machinery, but its weight and tire type would tear up our lawn," he replied, having returned to the section he was clearing.

Resigned to physical labour, Casey retrieved her shovel and changed the topic. "Is this going to become your new reading area?"

"Not new. Renewed. My reclining lawn chair is over there, leaning against the house. When you and the boys are at school, I often stop to take a break here, to watch the hummingbirds at the feeders, to read, to..."

"...snooze," Casey chimed in.

"Ha! Yes, that's happened a few times." He released an involuntary sigh as he looked around. "It's so peaceful here. I can envision the roses thriving and flourishing under the steady streams of sunrays, their splashes of colour a welcome addition to the bland landscape."

"Roses are such high maintenance plants. Why not chose other long-flowering perennials instead, like alliums and daisies? Has it to do with Mom?"

"Not intentionally, but maybe on a subconscious level it does. Roses were her favourite as they continually bloom, their scents so varied, so strong. I've come to appreciate them as much as she did. As for the maintenance, we'll plant some rose shrubs to cut down on the work, not that you need to worry about that end of things. This will be my hobby garden, and I look forward to nurturing it along."

"Sounds like a lovely way to unwind," she declared.

"You can participate whenever you'd like."

"How very thoughtful," she laughed. They carried on their work in silence, nature's symphony providing the background music: the rustling leaves, the black-capped chickadee calling from somewhere deep within the woods, and the steady tapping by the resident pileated woodpecker.

Tugging at a stubborn thistle, Casey asked, "Why didn't Grandpa like gardens?"

"What makes you think he didn't?"

She shook out the soil from an uprooted thistle before pitching it aside. "Grandpa never worked them. Us kids did, and you and mom did, but not him. Why was that?"

"Your grandpa was a man full of disappointments. He could never see what he had; he only saw what he didn't have. He felt he lived on the land Jeremiah described."

Casey bent over to pry loose a stone with her gloved hands. "Jeremiah?"

"Yes, the Book of Jeremiah, verse 17:6 to be exact. Grandpa should have mounted it on a plaque for the living room wall, but I suppose living on this land was reminder enough." Jeffrey rested an arm on the shovel's handle as he recited the part of the verse that had been quoted to him over the years: He 'will not see when prosperity comes, But will live in stony wastes in the wilderness.'" (NASB)

"But Grandpa didn't live in such a place."

Jeffrey smacked a hardened lump of soil with his shovel sending dirt in all directions. "I suppose he felt he was in a place similar to it. Grandpa viewed Rocky Meadows as worthless land, a stony waste. He tried selling it, but no one would buy it, not when there was lush farmland in the valley to be had.

"What about Great-Uncle Edward? Couldn't he have bought it?"

"Probably, and it would have been the ideal solution, especially since his land was right next door, but he neither wanted nor needed it. Besides, his hands were full managing his own farm," Jeffrey explained while simultaneously massaging his aching right arm. "My uncle was quite satisfied with the living he made from raising his livestock on his 'stony waste' of land, right up until his death. Sadly, no one could get your grandpa to see the prosperity he had."

Casey looked over to where their cattle and sheep grazed on the rugged terrain. "And what do you see, Dad?"

Jeffrey motioned for his daughter to take a break with him. Together they walked towards the house, where he retrieved his lawn chair and unfolded it. Casey found a shaded section of grass to lie down on. "You were asking what I saw in this place," he began, stretching out his tired limbs. "What I see is God's hand on this land and us. Our livestock have plenty of grass to feed on, and they drink from the stream that flows through our property. We have several pens filled with chickens and pigs and a vegetable garden that fills our freezer and canning shelves. We have the security of owning a home. And surrounding our property are our wonderful farming neighbours. We want for nothing." He reached for the water bottle he had placed under his chair. Unscrewing its lid, he took several sips of the ice-cold water, pouring some onto his bandana to cool his face and neck. "Do you remember the ceramic tile you painted in grade school?"

"Of course. I made it for Mother's Day," Casey said, recalling the square tile trivet they used at mealtimes for hot dishes.

Jeffrey looked tenderly at his eldest child. "That's right," he said, briefly reflecting on the fact that five years had passed since his beloved had died. Oh, how he missed her. Her heart was always filled with joy, committed to gratitude even in times of adversity. And it infected all those she connected with. She was a living example of the bible verse: 'for the joy of the Lord is your strength.' (Nehemiah 8:10 NIV). Yes, she was strong, right to the very end. Refocusing his attention to the present, he asked: "Why do you think we still have it?"

She stared up at the cloudless, blue sky. "Because we're extra careful with it."

"Uh-huh. And we're extra careful because we know it's special. You made it with love and gave it with love, so we handle it, with love." Jeffrey swept his hand before him. "This land is special to me. I love the memories it brings of your mom. I love it because I can raise my family on it. I love it because it reminds me of God's goodness. Love is the key ingredient."

Casey sighed as she pushed herself onto her elbows. "What I see are our cattle and sheep scattered across our rugged lands. And this dirt," kicking the ground with her heel, "if you can call it dirt, is full of rocks!"

"You're either grateful, or you're not. You can't be on the fence post, dear."

"You know I am, but everything seems to require double the effort, this rose garden being a case in point. The soil is so poor I'd be amazed if any plants grow, let alone survive another year."

Jeffrey raised his eyebrows. "And for that, you want to throw in the towel? Most things in life must be worked for, Casey. Trust me. You'll appreciate the fruits of your labour because of the sweat and love you invested in it. As for the soil, come on now, we're farmers with plenty of liquid manure to rototill into this nutrient-poor soil."

Looking over the partially upturned earth, Casey

dishearteningly responded, "Oh Dad, that'll take forever. We'll need oodles of roses to fill in such a huge area. Why not scale it down to half the size?"

"There's no need to, as we'll plant annuals as fillers. And it won't take forever, but it will take a few years. What happened to my optimistic Casey?"

"Trying to avoid manual labour whenever possible," she said half-seriously.

Jeffrey wiped the beads of sweat from his forehead with his bandana. Checking his wristwatch, he noted that lunchtime was in less than an hour. "Break time is over."

Reluctantly, Casey got up and headed towards the shovel she had speared into the dirt. She stomped onto the blade's step, forcing its edge deep into the ground. The earth was flipped over, revealing the hidden rocks, which were picked up and thrown into the wheelbarrow. She repeated these steps until her load limit was reached. Taking a tight grip of the wheelbarrow handles, she pushed it the short distance to the trailer. Only then, in the silence that followed, did she realize that she'd been working alone. Glancing around, she was surprised to find her father hadn't moved from his chair. "Are you going to work, Dad, or be an observer?" Concern was etched on her face as she watched him struggle to stand, followed by unsteady steps. His body suddenly went limp, collapsing to the ground. "Dad!" she screamed. Fervently she prayed as she dashed across the yard: "Jesus, please don't take him home!"

CHAPTER 2

Casey was on her knees beside her father's motionless body. "Dad! Dad!" she anxiously cried out while shaking his shoulders. Jeffrey's eyes slowly opened. "Oh, Dad!" she sobbed, her head falling onto his chest in relief. When he mumbled incoherent words, she raised her head, inclining an ear towards him in the hopes she could better understand what he was trying to say. Even after his second attempt, his words remained unclear. Frustrated, he used his left hand to squeeze hers, panic visible in his eyes. "I'm going for help! I'll be right back," she assured him. He blinked his eyes in acknowledgement.

She ran around the side of the house. Having caught a glimpse of the barn door closing, she sprinted towards it. It reopened with Jason carrying a heavy bag of feed. Over the sound of his quad's motor, she repeatedly yelled out his name. Only when she was within earshot did she get his attention.

"Can't you see I'm busy, Sis?" Jason retorted, chucking the feed into the quad's trailer.

She reached over for the key, shutting off the motor, as words came tumbling out. "It's Dad! He's fallen. We were working on the rose garden. Oh, Jason, I think he may have had a heart attack!"

Her brother's eyes widened. Immediately he hauled the feed bag out of the utility trailer, dropping it to the ground. "Get on," he ordered. She took the position behind him on the quad, straddling the seat and holding on to his waist as he sped off. Jason pulled up a few metres from where their father laid.

Casey seized her brother's sleeve the moment he got off the quad. "Wait! I need your cell phone to call 911. Mine is in the house." He dug it out from his front pant pocket, tossing it to her before darting off towards their father. Her hand shook as she tapped the three digits on the keypad.

Jason was grateful to find his father conscious and aware of his surroundings. As he spoke reassuring words to him, he half-listened to the replies his sister gave to the 911 operator. He turned a puzzled face towards her when the talking stalled, receiving a hand signal to wait as she concentrated on the voice on the other end. Seconds later, she announced that an ambulance was being dispatched. Jason turned to his father to voice his concern. "You know it will take forever for them to get here." Jeffrey gave a yes-blink. "I think we should meet the ambulance halfway, agreed?" Yes-blink again. Casey relayed this information to the 911 operator, who stated she'd be staying on the line until the emergency personnel arrived.

With the aid of his children, Jeffrey managed to get up and into the trailer. He sat on its metal floor, his back resting against a side panel. Beside him sat Casey, her slender body absorbing his weight as he leaned helplessly against her. They both lurched forward when Jason set the quad in motion. Casey's reflex action had her throwing an outstretched arm across her father's chest. Silently, Jeffrey pleaded to Jesus: Heal me, for my children's sake.

Jason parked the quad and trailer at the rear of the farm's

work truck, an older model half-ton pickup truck. His father had chosen the truck bed when given the option between it or the cab. It made sense, thought Jason, as he hastily pulled down the truck's tailgate. His father could either sit up with his legs outstretched or lay down, whichever was more comfortable. Racing to the barn, he fetched a hay bale to use as a makeshift step. He and Casey then assisted their father out of the utility trailer and onto it. From that height, Jeffrey was able to rest on the tailgate.

Casey remained with her father while Jason grabbed the bale's binding, hoisting it onto the truck bed. Flipping it on its side, he dragged it to the opposite end, shoving it into the far corner. He then leapt over the truck's side to retrieve a jacket from within the cab, throwing it on top of the bale. Returning to the tailgate, he and Casey helped their father struggle to his feet. Placing his arms around each of their necks, they held his wrist with one hand and his belt with the other. Supported in this manner, Jeffrey hobbled the short distance to the back of the truck bed, where he was eased down and propped against the bale. Casey reached for the jacket arranging it in such a way as to protect him from the coarse hay and dried stalk pieces. She parked herself tight against him; Jeffrey was securely sandwiched in for the trip.

Having closed the tailgate, Jason ran to the driver's side door, thrusting it open. "Tell the 911 operator we're heading out," he said. "We'll meet the ambulance by Grantham Corner Store."

"Hey, where are you going?" asked Aaron casually, having left the house with a granola bar in one hand and an apple in the other.

In all the excitement, they had forgotten about their twelve-year-old brother. Jason stood on the running board, gripping the top of the door. "Get in!" he motioned frantically. "We think Dad has had a heart attack!"

Aaron flung his snacks aside as he bolted across the driveway. Once inside the truck cab, he looked through the rear window where his father rested against a hale bale. Casey smiled wanly as she met his anxious eyes. In a voice that quivered, Aaron asked his brother what had happened.

"Get your seatbelt on!" came the sharp reply as Jason moved the gear into drive and pressed hard on the gas pedal. The tires spun gravel out from underneath as the pick-up truck took off down the long driveway. Once he had turned onto the rural road, he gave an account of what had transpired. Minutes later, he was accelerating on a paved secondary road, exceeding the posted speed limit by several kilometres.

"We're almost at Grantham Corner, but there's no ambulance," Casey reported to the 911 operator.

"There!" shouted Aaron. "They've just come around Carson Road's bend." Jason rolled the truck smoothly into Grantham Corner Store's parking lot; the ambulance pulled up beside them.

"The paramedics are here, Dad. Help has arrived," Casey said with relief.

"Then I'll leave you in their capable hands. Goodbye, Casey," said the 911 operator. She had momentarily forgotten about the operator being on the other end. The cell phone was stuffed into her jean pocket just as one of the attendants climbed onto the truck bed with a portable monitoring machine.

As the attendant hooked the cardiac leads onto Jeffrey's body, he simultaneously asked a series of questions. Noting his patient's difficulty with speech, he redirected the questions to Casey. The boys were absorbed with what the second attendant was engaged in - maneuvering a hydraulic lifting stretcher from the ambulance to the truck. When the stretcher had been locked into position, the second attendant leapt onto the truck bed to assist his partner.

The attendants, having determined Jeffrey was safe to be transported, deftly lifted him onto a stretcher board. They positioned his arms to his sides and adjusted the straps to secure him. "We're going to lift you from the truck onto a powered stretcher," an attendant explained to Jeffrey while placing the monitoring machine near his feet. "Ready?" Jeffrey blinked his affirmation. Once on the powered stretcher, the attendants temporarily unstrapped him to pull the stretcher board out. They then set to work to re-secure the straps over his shoulders, chest, pelvis, and legs. With Jeffrey securely buckled in, the attendants took hold of the stretcher's frame, pulling it towards the ambulance.

Casey had hopped over the side panel to stand alongside her brothers. Jason had an arm casually draped over Aaron's shoulder. They looked on in stunned silence as the attendants rolled the stretcher past them. Their father hadn't noticed them; his eyes were closed, his body eerily still. The first attendant shut the back doors on his patient and colleague. Facing his onlookers, he said, "We've room for one more if someone wants to ride in the front passenger seat."

"You go," Jason said, lightly pushing his sister forward. "We'll meet you at the hospital."

The ambulance's shrieking siren once again pierced the air as it sped down the highway towards Hawkview Hospital. Although Aaron urged his brother to keep up with it, Jason wisely followed the traffic laws. "They have the right-of-way and can go through red lights and intersections," he said. "We can't, not without risking our lives and others." Aaron stared at the ambulance as the span between them grew. "We'll be arriving not long after they do," Jason said in a calm tone that belied his uneasy feelings.

Inside the emergency department, a student nurse brought

the boys into the assessment area. They took their place beside Casey, mutely observing from a distance the flurry of activity from the healthcare team as they carried out the doctor's orders. The last order he gave was for the patient to be transported to the medical imaging department for a CT scan.

As Jeffrey was wheeled away by a nurse, the doctor removed and disposed of his medical gloves. When he turned around, he saw three young people approaching him. Why weren't they in the waiting room, he angrily wondered. What if a defibrillator had to be used on their father, or worse yet, what if he had died? They shouldn't have been here! Frowning, he motioned for the trio to follow him into an adjoining room. He'd sort this blunder out later with the nurse manager.

"I'm Dr. Orst, Resident Doctor." Casey introduced herself and her brothers. "Have a seat," he said, taking the chair nearest to him. "Wife?" he inquired.

"Widowed," replied Jason. "We're his family. He hasn't anyone else."

Dr. Orst gave them his qualifier smile, his go-to smile, as he relayed the facts void of emotions. "Your father has had a stroke. I've ordered various tests to find out what caused it. He's receiving medications that will help prevent another one. You already know that he's lost some abilities, like speech and strength. These are associated with his right-sided paralysis. He'll be admitted to an intensive care bed on our cardiac unit where staff will continue to monitor his vitals and assess the extent of his losses."

Casey asked the daunting question, the one she knew to be also on her brothers' minds. "Is our father going to die?"

"Not if we can help it," Dr. Orst replied. "We'll know more within the next 24 to 48 hours." He was sensitive to their feelings of frustration as he responded in generalities to their questions.

"It's not possible for me to be more specific, not until I know more of what's going on with him."

"We don't mean to sound ungrateful," Casey said. "It's just that the unknown is a scary place to be." The doctor understood, promising to keep them informed. "When can we see him?"

"It'll be a while. Why don't you go to the cafeteria and get a bite to eat? By the time you've finished, staff will have moved your father onto the cardiac unit."

"I'm waiting right here!" Aaron said, crossing his arms.

"No, not here, as this is a consultation room. I'll have someone bring you to the waiting area if that's your preference," said Dr. Orst as he stood up. He directed his final remarks to Jason and Casey: "Check in on the cardiac unit in half-an-hour, not any earlier. If he hasn't arrived, someone will direct you to the Quiet Room where you can wait." Three pairs of eyes watched him leave, the door closing silently behind him.

Casey caught Aaron wiping away a tear with his shirtsleeve. He needed a distraction. They all did. "It's well past lunch hour, and I haven't had anything to eat since breakfast. What do you say we go check out that cafeteria?"

"I'm with you," said Jason, having noted his brother's downcast gaze. "And don't tell me you're not hungry, Aaron, as I'm quite sure I saw you leave something behind for Harley." A sliver of a smirk emerged as Aaron pictured his Blue Heeler dog finding the unexpected treats. They left the organized chaos of the emergency department, following the wall signs to the cafeteria.

The cafeteria food court had multiple food and beverage vendors, making it tough for Aaron to decide which eatery to approach. In the end, he settled for his favourite - a double cheeseburger with fries. Having made their purchases, Casey led the way to a recently vacated table. As each deposited their tray and took a seat, a familiar voice interrupted them.

"What brings the Kallan family to my place of work? And where's your father?" Dr. Bleviss asked, surveying the people queued at the various counters.

"He's why we're here," Casey replied. She proceeded to tell their neighbour all that had happened.

Dr. Bleviss sat down beside Aaron, helping himself to some of his fries. "Your father has a lot going for him. He's strong physically, emotionally, and spiritually. Plus, he's in a great hospital."

"Because you're here?" Aaron asked in jest.

Dr. Bleviss chuckled. "Because this hospital has a state-of-the-art cardiac unit. It comes with a very competent cardiac team." Casey slid over her lemon pie, which he graciously accepted. "I'll escort you to the unit," he said, "when we've all finished eating." He winked at Aaron as he lifted a piece of pie to his mouth.

On the Cardiac Care Unit, Dr. Bleviss introduced the family to the charge nurse and asked if Mr. Kallan had arrived. He had. The doctor took a few minutes to read Jeffrey's chart, then lightly pushed the three young people forward. "They won't stay long," he promised as he whisked them inside their father's room before the nurse had a chance to reprimand him for breaking the one-visitor-only rule.

"Jeffrey," Dr. Bleviss called out, gently tapping his arm. Eyes fluttered open. "Hello, my friend. You're in the intensive care unit. Do you know that?" Jeffrey nodded, clearly agitated that his spoken words came out garbled. "And Dr. Orst told you what's happened?" Again, he nodded, giving a reassuring albeit lopsided smile to his daughter and sons.

"Good. Your children are aware that they can only stay for a few minutes." He signalled for them to draw nearer.

Jeffrey noted that each of his children tried to remain stoic as he received their kisses and hugs. Only in Aaron did he see the glistening wet eyes. They were afraid. A part of him was too. Silently he pleaded to the Holy Spirit: Intercede for me, for I feel like I'm drowning in a sea of emotions.

Dr. Bleviss took hold of Jeffrey's hand. "I'll be by often to check in on you, my friend. Get some rest. As I was telling your children earlier, you're in a state-of-the-art cardiac unit. You're in good hands, both on the ground and from up above," he said, raising his eyes fleetingly heavenward. "Come, you three. We best leave or else the charge nurse will scold me for having exceeded the visitor restriction limit."

"Well?" asked Casey of Dr. Bleviss as soon as the automatic doors to the intensive care unit closed behind them. Dr. Bleviss didn't respond. Instead, he guided them to the Quiet Room, currently void of any visitors. Casey and the doctor chose to sit on the padded chairs while Jason and Aaron took a seat on the sofa. "How serious is it?" she asked.

"And don't bother sugar-coating it!" advised Jason, with Aaron vigorously bobbing his head beside him.

"It's too soon to know anything," Dr. Bleviss replied.

Casey placed a hand on his wrist. "Please," she begged.

The doctor gave an understanding smile. "Okay," he said, patting her hand. "Your father has had a life-threatening stroke, which means he'll remain in the ICU so that a careful watch can be kept on him. If there are no changes in the next few days, he'll be transferred to our rehabilitation wing. There they'll work with him to get his strength, mobility and speech back."

Casey's forehead creased. "What did you mean when you said, 'if there are no changes.' Dr. Bleviss looked at each of them, his eyes resting longer on young Aaron. Casey raised her eyebrows. "We all need to know."

"Yes, of course," Dr. Bleviss said, uncrossing his legs and laying his clasped hands on them. "Being on an intensive care unit means that a patient requires constant monitoring and support. Should something change, staff can intervene quickly. In your father's case, they're monitoring for atrial fibrillation, which is an irregular heartbeat, as there's a chance he may experience another stroke."

"How much of a chance?" Jason was quick to ask.

"Studies have shown that a second stroke can occur within the first couple of days of the initial one. That's why your father is on this unit, hooked up to all the machines. He'll be receiving around-the-clock monitoring."

"And if he doesn't have this second stroke, then what happens?" inquired Casey.

"First, the team completes a thorough assessment to determine how much damage the stroke caused, then they'll come up with a treatment plan. Once your father is deemed stable, he'll start his therapies on the rehab unit. His progress will be dependent on the parts of his mind and body that can heal and on his willingness to get better."

"And on God," added Casey.

"Absolutely," agreed Dr. Bleviss. "So. Who's staying?"

"It has to be Casey as she doesn't have her driver's license with her," Jason said. "Aaron, you and I will take care of the farm chores and come back and see Dad tomorrow. Okay, buddy?"

Aaron shrugged his shoulders. "I guess."

"At-a-boy," he said, giving his brother a gentle body shove. "When we get home, I need you to place a tarp over that 45 kg bag of seed I dropped by the barn door while I check on the herd."

"I'll do better than that. I'll drag it into the barn!" he said, flexing an arm.

Casey and Jason both laughed. They knew their brother

couldn't lug the bag himself, but he was clever enough to find a way to get it indoors.

"Let's pray before we part ways," Casey suggested as she moved her chair closer to Jason and Aaron. Dr. Bleviss did the same. With heads bowed, she offered up their petition. "Heavenly Father, we ask that you make your presence known to Dad. Quieten any fears he may have. Comfort him during this trying time. We ask for divine healing, for you are the great physician. Bless all who care for him, be they health care professionals, cleaners, or volunteers. And be with us, Lord. Calm our hearts and give us the peace that passes understanding. We ask this in Jesus' name. Amen."

As they stood, Dr. Bleviss gave a fatherly squeeze to Casey's shoulder. "Have me paged if you need me. Come with me, you two. I'll accompany you to the front entrance."

"Call me if anything changes or if you just want to talk," Jason said, hugging his sister. "I'll bring your phone and wallet in tomorrow."

Aaron hugged her too, holding on a little tighter and for a little longer. "Can I call you tonight?" he asked in a pained whisper.

"Absolutely. I want to hear what Jason ends up feeding you for supper."

"I can already tell you what's on the menu," Jason said. "Potatoes and juicy pork chops on the barbecue. You can help with the grilling, Aaron."

"There will be no mouthwatering pork chops if you both don't get a move on," joked Dr. Bleviss. While the boys left with the doctor, Casey returned to the ICU, stopping at the desk to request a cot be placed in her father's room.

The following days passed in a blur. Staff were in and out of Jeffrey's room, drawing blood, assessing his swallowing abilities, repositioning him to prevent bedsores, sending him for another CT scan, and a host of other things to monitor progress and setbacks. Casey and Jason alternated between sitting with their father and completing farm chores, in addition to being pseudo-parents to their younger brother and completing school assignments. During their shift change, Aaron spent time alone with their father while his siblings went to the cafeteria to update one another. They discussed many things, choosing to avoid the topics neither wished to contemplate - a second stroke or him dying. They held on to hope as they observed his small gains: his headaches were gone, he could walk a few steps, and he was more alert. And so, their prayers for healing continued.

On the fourth day of Jeffrey's hospital admission, Casey entered her father's room to find an orderly transferring him into a wheelchair. "What's going on?" she asked as she embraced her father. "He doesn't have any tests scheduled for today. Is something wrong?"

"Quite the opposite," said a young man entering the room wearing a white lab coat with the Hawkview Hospital logo embroidered on it. "I'm Caleb, his physical therapist, PT for short. And you are?"

"Casey, his daughter," she said, extending her hand.

"Well, Casey, your father is being transferred to the rehabilitation wing where he'll begin an exercise regimen." Caleb thanked the orderly before taking hold of the wheelchair handles and pushing it forward. "His hemiparesis has caused right-sided weakness. We're going to try to recoup those damaged areas. Isn't that right, Mr. Kallan?"

"Yes," Jeffrey replied in a slurred voice.

Try to recoup damaged areas? What did he mean by that, Casey wondered as she kept pace alongside Caleb? And then it hit her; her father may never fully recover! She looked over at him, the visible effects of the stroke quite apparent: hunched posture, clenched right fist, foot drop. No, don't think such defeatist thoughts, she admonished herself.

Caleb made his way through the mazes of hallways and corridors. "That's your new hospital entry point, Casey," he said, as they wheeled around visitors, patients, and staff who were also negotiating their way through the large foyer. "Would you?" Caleb asked, pointing to the handicap push plate button on the wall. Casey pressed it, the automatic doors opening in response. Once inside the rehab unit, Caleb reached for the chart that Jeffrey carried on his lap, depositing it onto the nursing station's counter in passing. "Your new, temporary, home," he announced as Jeffrey was wheeled into the semi-private room.

"Seriously, Caleb?" came the agitated male voice from behind the curtained partition. "I don't even get to have the room to myself for one day?"

"And hello to you too, Brandon. Jeffrey Kallan is your new roommate. His daughter, Casey, is here as well. Can you be polite and show yourself?"

"Nope."

"Well, you might want to at some point," Caleb said as he set the brakes on the wheelchair before assisting Jeffrey to the bed. "You two have a few things in common."

"Doubt it."

Caleb switched the bed and light controls from the right side of the bed to the left. "We'll be working on muscle stretching and strengthening to regain function to your dominate hand." He checked his watch. "After lunch, I'll have a porter bring you to the Physio Clinic. See you soon. Nice to meet you, Casey."

With Caleb gone, Casey pulled up a chair beside her father. "Do you want to rest, Dad, or would you like me to read to you?"

"Read."

She held up a novel and a Bible as choices. With great effort, Jeffrey raised his right hand and tapped the Bible weakly with his knuckles.

"Any particular passage?"

"Philip." And because he had trouble naming the verse, he used his left hand to raise four fingers."

"Okay, Philippians 4." Turning to the passage, Casey scanned the verses. "I'll start at verse 10. 'Thanks for Their Gifts. I rejoiced greatly in the Lord that at last you renewed your concern for me. Indeed, you were concerned, but you had no opportunity to show it. I am not saying this because I am in need, for I have learned to be content whatever the circumstances.'" (Phil. 4:10-11NIV)

"Seriously?" muttered Brandon from behind the drapes. "Take your dad and read it someplace else!"

Casey gave a playful smile to her father as she responded with one word: "Nope."

"Oh, come on! You can't believe that garbage you're reading?"

"You know the saying, one man's trash is another man's treasure." Jeffrey stifled a chuckle. "The door is open should *you* want to leave." As there was no stirring from the bed across from them, she resumed her reading: "'I know what it is to be in need, and I know what it is to have plenty. I have learned the secret of being content in any and every situation, whether well fed or hungry, whether living in plenty or in want. I can do all this through him who gives me strength. Yet it was good of you to share in my troubles. Moreover, as you Philippians know, in the early days of your acquaintance with the gospel, when I set out from Macedonia, not one church shared with me in the matter of giving and receiving, except you only; for even when I was in Thessalonica, you sent me aid more than once when I was in need. Not that I desire your gifts; what I desire is that more be credited to your account. I have received full payment and have more than enough. I am amply supplied, now that I have received from Epaphroditus the gifts you sent. They are a fragrant offering, an acceptable sacrifice, pleasing to God. And my God will meet all your needs according to the riches of his glory in Christ Jesus. To our God and Father be glory forever and ever. Amen.'" (Phil. 4:12-20 NIV)

"Hallelujah!" came the snide response.

"Hallelujah, indeed!" responded Casey. A food service worker brought in the lunch trays, preventing her from saying more. Having prayed a blessing over his meal, she took the lid off the soup bowl and picked up the spoon.

"Me," Jeffrey said, extending his left arm to receive the spoon into his open palm. He then transferred it to his clenched right hand. Raising his electric bed to a more comfortable level, he signalled to Casey to bring the overhead table closer.

She snapped the adult mealtime bib around his neck and watched the effort exerted to feed himself. "Are you sure you don't want help?"

"Let your dad be. He's not going to improve if you do it for him, now is he?"

Brandon was right. "Sorry, Dad," she said in a low, sullen voice. Retrieving her lunch bag from her backpack, she said, "I'm going to the cafeteria so you can eat at your own pace and without an audience. Can I get you anything?" Her father mumbled, 'no.' "What about you, Brandon?"

"Since you're accepting orders, I'll have one of those puffed wheat squares."

"One of my favourites. I'll be back in half-an-hour," she said to her father and the curtain that closeted Brandon. The cafeteria was crowded because it was the lunch hour. She stood in line to order a bowl of soup and another line for the puffed wheat square. Having determined her father would be with the PT by the time she returned, she headed for an empty table to enjoy her simple meal in solitude.

As predicted, Jeffrey was not in the room when she re-entered it. "Brandon?" No answer. Casey hesitantly approached the curtain, calling out his name one more time before slowly pulling it back. He was out too. She lifted his flattened pillow giving it a few gentle shakes to plump it up before laying the puffed wheat square in its centre.

She was drawing the curtains closed when she spotted the edge of a book lying beneath a magazine on his bedside table. Curious about what he was reading, she glanced over her shoulder to ensure the coast was clear then nudged the magazine aside. When the word 'Stone' began to glow from the book's title 'Sticks and Stones around the Globe,' Casey caught her breath. The hairs on her arms still bristled as she looked around again, this time hoping someone had been present. But there was no one. Probably just as well, having stepped cautiously forward and finding nothing special happening with the title. "That was no figment of my imagination!" she said as she slid the magazine back atop the book.

At the nurses' station, Casey inquired how long her father would remain with the PT. "Hard to know as they work with them according to their level of tolerance," reported the unit clerk. She returned to her father's room and unzipped her backpack, withdrawing a pen, notepad and a school textbook. Her father's overhead table would serve as her study desk until he returned.

The room was quiet until Brandon drove his powered wheelchair into it. "Casey, I assume," he said in a flat tone while negotiating his wheelchair alongside the edge of his bed, parking it at a slight angle. The thirty-something-year-old had a left-hand amputation, the stump wrapped in gauze, and a below-the-knee cast on his left leg.

"When does the cast come off?" she inquired.

He stood on his good foot, hopped a couple of steps away from the chair, pivoted, then sat down on his bed. "What business is it of yours?" he snapped as he scooted further back onto the bed to bring the casted leg onto it.

"It's a general question," replied Casey. "You know, polite conversation. Would you rather I ask about the weather?"

"How about you don't ask anything at all!" he said, yanking the curtain closed.

Casey heard the crinkling sound of plastic wrap, but she received not a word of thanks for the snack she purchased. Then again, she didn't buy the square to receive his gratitude. She just wanted to. No, that wasn't entirely true. She bought it in the hopes Brandon would talk to her. He seemed angry. Was it the injury or something else, she wondered as she recalled the book's title: Sticks and Stones around the Globe.

When Casey's father returned, his mood wasn't much better than Brandon's. He suggested she go home as he was tired and wanted to rest, but she refused to leave. Instead, she gathered her study materials and headed for the floor's Quiet Room. She prayed that he'd be in better spirits when she returned. He wasn't.

CHAPTER 3

It was 6:30 in the morning when Jason entered the house, tossing his jacket onto the coat hook and his worn ball cap onto the bench below it. He headed straight down the hall for a much-needed shower to remove the grime and smells from the barn stalls. When he walked into the kitchen, he was promptly put to work.

"Juice needs to go on the table," Casey said as she removed the browned slices from the toaster.

He opened the refrigerator, sliding aside the milk jug to reach the orange juice carton. "It's been a couple of weeks since Dad's stroke," he said, closing the door with the heel of his foot and placing the one-litre carton on the counter. "Some of our farm supplies need to be replenished."

Casey used a slotted ladle to lift the eggs from the pot of boiling water, carefully transferring them into a bowl. "There's no sense talking to Dad about it as he's not interested. Whenever I bring things up, he assures me that you and I can figure it out." She poured steaming hot water from the kettle into the teapot, the water turning colour from the dried green tea leaves within the tea infuser. With the plate of toast in one hand and the bowl of eggs in the other, she carried the items to the kitchen table. "Bring the teapot, will you? And the juice," she said over her shoulder. Casey placed the hot eggs into the egg cup holders while Jason laid his items on the table. "Buy whatever supplies are needed using the farm credit card. You'll find it in Dad's desk drawer."

Seeing that all was ready, Jason headed down the hall to rap on Aaron's door. "Breakfast, buddy."

Aaron prayed over their meal. His "Amen" had barely left his mouth when his hand reached out for a slice of toast. "Don't you think Dad would do better if he were at home?" he asked while buttering his toast.

Casey was slicing the top off her egg. "Maybe. He does seem to be in a slump. Being home might help him get out of it."

"Or he'd become more depressed seeing all the things he's unable to do," Jason said while pouring himself a glass of orange juice.

"It may motivate him to try," Casey countered.

"Or it may make it worse," Jason fired back. "Besides, Dad will need help when he gets home, and I can't take on any more responsibilities. I'm already struggling to keep on top of my schoolwork."

"What are you saying?" asked Aaron, looking uneasily from one sibling to the other. "Is Dad never coming home?"

"No, no. That's not what Jason is saying at all. He means that we can't be Dad's full-time caregivers. Remember when Dad was in the ICU? One of us was always with him, while the other two took on the household and farm responsibilities. Jason and I had to miss school, and you had to take on additional chores to help out. Those were emotionally and physically exhausting days. Thankfully, Dad stabilized. He was moved to the rehab unit, which meant we no longer needed to be there 24/7. Jason and I could return to school. But the work at home hasn't changed for any of us.

"Aaron, if Dad came home today, we might find ourselves as exhausted as those ICU days. At the hospital, he has staff to help him get dressed and undressed, his meals and snacks are brought to him, and his therapists are on-site. If he came home, we'd have to help him with all those things, plus drive him to and from appointments," said Casey. "For Dad to come home, we would need to hire help, which we can't afford to do." Her eyes slowly widened. "He has health insurance! It must offer some type of home care assistance."

"I don't know," said Jason. "It'll still be a lot for us to handle. Home Care isn't going to stay with him all day."

"We could line up volunteers," suggested Casey, "to plug some of the gaps between what home care offers and what we can do." The remainder of their breakfast time was spent identifying potential helpers. Things looked brighter, even from Jason's perspective, as the possibility of their father coming home seemed doable.

At the hospital, Casey greeted her father with a warm hug. She noted the absence of Brandon's power wheelchair. "Is he at therapy?"

Jeffrey nodded. "He should be back soon."

His speech remained slurred, so how was it that she had no trouble understanding him? Did it mean he was improving or had she adjusted to his new speech pattern? Let it be the former, Casey silently prayed. She was pleased that Brandon was out, for she wasn't in the mood for any of his sarcastic comments. Lifting her father's housecoat off the plastic chair, she laid it on his bed before drawing it closer to his wheelchair.

Jeffrey reached for her hand. "What's wrong?"

"Nothing's wrong. Not really. We miss you, Dad. We want you to come home." In a voice that bubbled over with excitement, she shared the breakfast conversation. "I think it's possible, don't you?"

"What's possible?" asked Dr. Bleviss as he and a young male intern entered the room. The intern was introduced as Dr. Hastings.

"Having my dad come home," Casey said, beaming. "My brothers and I discussed it this morning. We feel we can manage, with the help of home care services and volunteers." With a broad grin, she looked back at her father. "You would have meals with us, sit in your favourite chair, and sleep in your own bed. Home, Dad! Doesn't that sound awesome?" She was interrupted by the buzzing sound from her cell phone. Having viewed the number displayed, she said, "It's my teacher, likely calling about my assignment. I've got to take it. I'll be back in a few minutes."

Dr. Bleviss sat in the vacated chair. "It's too soon to be talking discharge."

"I can do it with the kids' help," Jeffrey said to reassure him.

"Oh, I know they will, but at what cost? Casey is studying for her grade 12 exams, Jason his grade 11 exams, and this is in addition to taking care of Aaron, the farm work, the housework, and everything else in between. They love you, Jeffrey. That much is obvious. Would it be fair to ask them to care for your needs on top of everything else they're doing?"

He lowered his eyes and shook his head.

"Okay, thanks," were Casey's last words into the phone as she re-entered the room that had become ominously quiet. Her eyes narrowed. "Dad?"

It was Dr. Bleviss who spoke. "Your father has decided to remain here to carry on with his therapy." Jeffrey gave her a weak smile.

She turned angry eyes on Dr. Bleviss, then on Dr. Hastings, and back onto her neighbour. "You talked him into staying, didn't you? Why would you do that to him?"

"If you wouldn't mind waiting in the Quiet Room," interrupted Dr. Hastings. "We'll send someone for you when we're done."

She didn't acknowledge Dr. Hastings; her eyes remained locked on Dr. Bleviss. "Well?"

"Casey, you and the boys came up with some creative ideas to manage my care at home, but it's premature," her father resignedly said. "The time will come, dear. Now please, do what Dr. Hastings requested."

How could they be deaf to his defeatist tone? Glaring at Dr. Bleviss, she furiously said: "I thought you'd advocate for what was best for my dad! He needs to be with his family, at home!" The doctors weren't the only recipients of her glowering eyes; her father was, too. He had yielded; he hadn't engaged in a defensive argument. "Fine, Dad. I'll leave," she said, storming out of the room.

Dr. Bleviss moved his chair an inch closer. "She's right, you know. You do belong at home."

"Your progress has been good," reflected Dr. Hastings as he read the staffs' medical notes on his tablet. "But, it's not where it should be by this time. Are you depressed? I'm reading that they've suggested counselling, but you've refused."

Dr. Bleviss lightly shook his head in disbelief at the bluntness of Dr. Hastings's approach.

"No counsellor!" Jeffrey firmly stated. "I can figure this out myself."

"It's not unusual to feel despondent as you grieve the changes your stroke has caused," Dr. Hastings continued.

"You don't think I know that! I'm not a stranger when it

comes to having experienced loss, thank you very much!" Jeffrey drew in a deep breath, slowly releasing it. "I seem to be fighting with everyone these days." He took another calming breath. "Mostly with God."

Dr. Bleviss raised a questioning eyebrow at Dr. Hastings, who was clearly at a loss as to how to respond. He rescued him by asking a simple question. "And how's the battle going, my friend?"

"Not well. I think He sent you to attack me from a different front."

"You're wrong, Jeffrey. We're not fighting against you; we're fighting with you. We're on the same side," Dr. Bleviss stressed.

"It doesn't feel like that when PT staff pressure me to do things I can't do. I feel like a failure."

"You're not," assured Dr. Bleviss. "The team has the bar for success set at a high level because they feel you can reach it. Your utmost effort is required, not your half-hearted attempts."

"I have been giving it my all!"

"Are you saying that's all you got? Because if it is, then you might as well throw in the towel and go home."

Jeffrey clenched his jaw. "I didn't say I was quitting!"

"Then try harder. Don't accept defeat!" Dr. Bleviss counselled. "And yes, you will experience a rollercoaster of emotions, feelings of hopelessness, guilt, and apathy. They're to be expected. They're temporary, not the norm. And don't be so hard on yourself or Him. You know He's on your side, always."

"Who needs a therapist when I've got you?" Jeffrey conceded with an amused smile. Raising his left hand, he said, "I promise to make more of an effort by directing my frustrations elsewhere, likely at Caleb."

Dr. Bleviss patted his friend's knee. "I'm sure he can take it."

Casey had decided to go for a walk to destress. When she

returned, the room was empty, except for her father, who was typing something into his tablet. She sat down; her crestfallen face summed up her emotions. "Sorry for the outburst, Dad."

"I know you are. I'm sorry, too."

"What have you got to be sorry about?"

"For not giving it my all. I've been afraid of working too hard on my exercises, thinking it may cause another stroke. I've been caught up with the fear of dying, leaving the three of you all alone. I've been resentful at God for a myriad of things. I realized I've been sulking and ungrateful, mirroring your grandpa's attitude." Jeffrey handed his tablet to her. "I started a gratefulness list. Go ahead. Read it."

"Jesus loves me. Cassandra, Jason, Aaron. Beliefs and values instilled in my children. Being alive. Memory intact. Bathroom on my own." Casey laughed at the last one but also realized how challenging it must be for him to manage self-care tasks.

Her father took back the tablet. "I'm not done yet," he quietly affirmed. Casey's eyes moistened, knowing he wasn't referring to his list. Gazing up at the wall clock, Jeffrey mentioned that the porter would be coming in a few minutes to take him for some stress tests. "Do you want to study here?" He had guessed her plans correctly, judging from her reaction. "I read the textbook spine in your bag. I'm sure you didn't bring it for casual reading, especially as it's your least favourite subject."

"I don't think algebra is anyone's favourite," she laughed, picking up her bag.

"It's mine," professed Brandon as he hobbled into the room, his cast replaced with a walking boot. He appeared to move a little slower, looked a little paler.

"Are you okay?" she asked.

Plopping himself down on his bed, he released an exhausted

sigh. "The exercises seemed especially challenging today. How were they for you, Jeffrey?"

Casey looked from one to the other. "Oh, so you're on friendly talking terms, are you?"

Brandon looked across at his roommate. "We've had some restless nights, haven't we? And since we were both awake, it was only natural we should talk."

Casey stared suspiciously at Brandon. "Hmmm. Natural for you to talk. You, the one who barely speaks from his hideout."

"It's true," her father said. "We were talking about technological advances, and somehow it led to a discussion of modern farm equipment. A commonality emerged as we learned we were both raised on a farm. Brandon shared that his parents own and operate a large potato farm on Prince Edward Island. I shared our cattle and sheep farm business."

"I've never liked farm life," conceded Brandon. He turned over onto his side, drawing the covers over him. "Is it cold in here, or is it just me?"

Jeffrey, wearing a tee-shirt, shook his head. "Seems okay to us," Casey replied as she walked towards the thermostat on the wall. "Temperature remains at 21."

"Then it's me," muttered Brandon from under his blankets.

The porter came to take Jeffrey for his scheduled tests. If time permitted, he planned to stop in at the Physio Clinic for another workout. Casey moved to her familiar spot by the window. She opened her textbook, flipping to the chapter on linear functions. Oh, how she disliked algebra. Please help me make sense of this, she silently prayed.

An hour later, Casey stood to stretch her muscles. Outside, rain pelted against the windows. Brandon slept, but it was a restless sleep as he tossed and turned numerous times. Pulling her wallet from her purse, she decided to take a trip to the lower level to visit the now-familiar cafeteria to enjoy a bowl of butternut chicken soup.

She hadn't stepped a foot past Brandon's bed when she noticed the familiar book on his bedside table. It must be quite the book if he was still reading it, she thought, or perhaps it was his go-to book, as the Bible was hers. Her ponderings were delaying the real motive behind her desire to see the book – to find a rational explanation for what she had seen the first time she'd picked it up. Maybe the publisher used a graphic editor program, like Photoshop, to create a neon text effect for the title. Perhaps that's why the word in the title appeared to glow. She stealthy approached the bed, giving a sidelong glance at Brandon. She saw he slept soundly; his body cocooned within a hospital blanket. Cautiously the book was lifted only to be dropped like a hot object as the 'Stone' word suddenly shimmered from its cover. The thump of it hitting the floor awakened Brandon.

Rolling over, he dozily asked: "What was that?" When his heavy eyelids lifted and his blurry vision cleared, he demanded to know why she was at his bedside.

Casey didn't answer either question. Instead, she became alarmed at the sight of sweat beads on his face and his drenched hair. "You're burning up, Brandon. I'm getting the nurse," she said, beelining it to the nursing station. A lot of commotion soon followed. Casey tried to remain inconspicuous at her window seat as various staff entered and exited the room. Although she couldn't see what was going on because they worked behind the privacy curtain, she could hear all that was said.

Dr. Hastings strode into the room, slipping between the opening of the curtains. He instructed the nurse to remove the gauze bandages. "Ah, just as I suspected. You've got quite the infection brewing at the amputation site, Brandon. We're going to start you on an IV drip for fluids and antibiotics. You should feel an improvement within the next few days." He gave the nurse directions for the type and dose of antibiotics and pain medications to be administered through the IV. "I'll check on you later today." The nurse re-bandaged Brandon's stump and inserted an IV into his forearm. Not long after, the room fell silent.

"Casey?"

"I'm here, Brandon."

"Can you get me another blanket? I can't seem to get warm enough." As she laid the blanket over him, he asked: "Why were you at my bedside?"

How was she to answer that question? With the truth came the voice from within her. Yes, of course. One lie would lead to another. "It was your book, 'Sticks and Stones around the Globe,'" she confessed.

"Are you questioning why I would be reading something like that? Do you think I'm disturbed or have unresolved childhood bullying issues or something to that effect?"

"No! No!" she assured him. "Nothing like that at all!"

"Good to know. The book isn't about psychology; it's about archaeology. Life during the Middle Ages."

"Oh, I see. You're a fan of ancient history."

"And you're not, it would seem. If it wasn't the book's content that drew you to it, what was it?"

"It's just that, hmmm, how do I say this as it's going to sound very bizarre?" She decided to plunge right into the matter. "The title glowed. Well, actually, it was only one word in the title: Stones. It literally glowed from the cover!"

Reaching for the book, he asked, "Should I be taking your temperature?"

"Weird, right? But, I can't deny what I saw!"

Brandon was examining the book's cover. "Yeah, it's not

possible. Just like those three guys who were tossed into a furnace by a king and walked out of it, unharmed. That wasn't possible either."

"Are you sure about that?" asked Casey. "Sometimes you have to believe in the impossible when there's no other explanation. It's called a miracle. And the story you're referring to is about Daniel's friends, Shadrach, Meshach, and Abednego. They got thrown into a blazing furnace for refusing to bow down and worship King Nebuchadnezzar's gold statue. It's recorded in the Bible, chapter three of the Book of Daniel. The king had made a law demanding his people acknowledge the god he made of gold or else face execution by being pitched into a scorching furnace. The three refused, claiming there was only one true God. The king expected to witness screaming, burning bodies when the soldiers tossed them into the raging furnace. Instead, he sees three men walking about, joined by a fourth one, an angel. The king shouts to them from the mouth of the furnace to come out, and when they do, he finds their bodies and clothes unscathed from the fire. What does the king do then? He gives praise to their God and writes a new law punishing anyone who says anything against the God of Shadrach, Meshach, and Abednego."

"Uh-huh. Amazing story. Look, it doesn't matter to me if that story is true or not, just like I don't care whether you did or didn't see a word glow from this book's cover. What I do know is that if it hadn't been for you nosing around, I wouldn't have received the intervention when I did. So, how I see it, I owe you."

"That's not how I see it. I see it as a God-send."

"Naturally, you would," he said, passing the book to Casey to return to the side table. Not wanting to discuss gods, he changed the subject. "When's your algebra exam?"

"The middle of May," she said, relieved he wasn't pursuing

the title matter further. "Not a lot of time to understand the math equations and memorize the formulas."

"Understanding the formulas will give you the edge," Brandon said. "It'll take some time for the formula in this bag to work its magic on me, though. Once it has, I'd like to offer my services as a tutor."

"My personal tutor. How great is that?" declared Casey.

"Not so quick. There's a price attached to my service." He smiled inwardly when her shoulders slumped. "Aw, you can afford it."

She doubted it, knowing what she had in her bank account. "What's your fee?"

"Depends on how much a steady supply of homemade puffed wheat squares cost."

"Hmmm," Casey murmured as she tapped her lips with her index finger. "Butter is expensive, and so is cocoa powder, and..." Brandon held up his hand to stop the barrage of ingredients from being listed. She gave him a high-five in response. "Deal!"

"Good. Now get out of here as I need my beauty rest," he said on a yawn. "And close my door, will you?" With the drapes drawn around Brandon's bed, Casey retreated to the cafeteria to provide him with solitude.

"Can I join you?" Caleb asked, standing beside Casey's table with the packaged sandwich and drink he recently purchased. She motioned to the empty chair as she brought a spoonful of butternut chicken soup to her mouth. "How's your studying going?" he asked as he slipped into the seat across from her.

"You know about my upcoming exams?"

Caleb peeled back the cellophane from the triangular sandwich container. "Your father mentioned it during one of his workouts. We do talk about things besides muscle aches and pains."

"Yes, it stands to reason as my father wouldn't want his weaknesses to be the focal point of conversations." She finished off her soup before continuing. "You asked about my studies. I'm struggling with one particular subject as I don't understand the concepts. I wish I were smart, but I'm not. I'm average, plain and simple."

"Then you're in the majority," Caleb said as he took a bite of his sandwich.

"But I don't want to be!"

"Casey, being average doesn't define a person. What does is how they use their natural talents and spiritual gifts. You're a kind, giving, and compassionate person. You don't get marks for that, at least not in school. Where you get it is in life. You won't receive A's or B's, but you'll receive thanks, hugs, words of appreciation, and friendships. Believe me when I say that you have above-average abilities."

She sighed heavily. "I appreciate your kind words, but the fact remains that being average won't get me into university. It's why I decided on a gap year as I need time to figure out if going to university is the right direction for me. Regardless of whether I go, I need to pass all my exams to receive my high school diploma. It's the math exam I'm worried about, specifically the algebra portion of it. Brandon has offered to tutor me. I just hope it's not too late."

"You'll do fine. Do you want to know how I know? Because algebra is only a fraction of the exam. Hey, did you get that pun?" Her pursed lips and shaking head conveyed what she thought of it. "Well, I thought it was funny. Anyway, what I'm trying to say is for you not to spend all your time on it at the expense of the sections you're knowledgeable on."

She rested against the back of her chair. "Focus on what I know as that's where the majority of my marks will come from."

"Exactly. No one is ever 100% average; everyone excels at something." Caleb left her to mull over his remarks as he returned to the Physio Clinic.

At home, Casey filled Jason and Aaron in on their father's progress. She shared his worries and fears. She shared his gratefulness list and his resolve to apply himself more to the exercises. Hope was in the air.

Unfortunately, Brandon's hopes were tanking. The next time Casey crossed paths with him was when he was being wheeled down the hallway on a stretcher. He had placed an arm over his bleary eyes when he'd caught sight of her. She joined her father, who stood watching from the entranceway of his room. "What's happened?"

Jeffrey's eyes followed the stretcher until it disappeared around the corner. "The antibiotics aren't working," he said, staring down the empty hallway. A shiver went up Casey's spine. "I overheard Dr. Hastings say they'd be amputating below the elbow, higher if necessary." He turned to his daughter. "Come. We need to talk to Jesus."

CHAPTER 4

Casey noted that Brandon's belongings had been removed when she entered the familiar hospital room. "He's back on the medical ward," Jeffrey said as she sat down on his empty bed.

"Have you heard anything?"

"They're not going to share with us. We're not his family."

"Yeah, about that. Why aren't they here, Dad?"

"Not a clue. Do you know who else is missing? His friends. Brandon insists on having no visitors. And now that he's in a private room, he's added us to that list."

Casey heaved a sigh. "He's shutting out the world. I'll try to sneak in a visit to find out how he's doing and why he's chosen seclusion. He might let me in when he finds out what I brought him."

She entered the medical ward that afternoon, casually walking down the hall towards Brandon's room. When his door opened, she pretended to be absorbed with the contents of the small bag she carried. A lab technician exited with his phlebotomy cart. When he passed her, she quickly stepped inside the room.

Brandon was lying on his bed, listening to music. A taped cotton ball on his arm indicated his recent blood donation. "I see you got past my nursing guards," he said, removing his earbuds and setting his phone aside.

"I'm sure they have more important duties to attend to," she said, smiling widely. "Besides, I don't think you'll want to send me away unless you'd rather not have these," she said, waving a small bag before him. "They come from the Kallan kitchen."

Brandon snatched the bag from her and peeked inside it. "Okay, you can stay." He withdrew a granola bar and an extra-large puffed wheat square, laying them on his bedside table.

"How did the surgery go?"

Brandon whipped back the bedsheet to reveal the below-elbow amputation.

"Oh," she gasped.

He re-covered the stump with the sheet. "I kind of expected it," he confided. "I had been forewarned the surgery could lead to other complications, such as a wound infection. I had hoped the powerful antibiotics they'd given me would have done the trick. I suppose I should be grateful as it slowed the infection down, preventing more of my arm from being amputated. Ah, what does it even matter? It's not as if they could salvage my career."

Casey pulled up a chair. "Career in what?"

"Music. I play the trumpet. Played," Brandon corrected.

"You're in a band?"

"Not anymore. I have no idea what I'm going to do now."

Casey smiled. "Besides being a potato farmer."

He smirked. "Yeah, besides that. My parents sacrificed much to send me to university. What a waste of schooling!"

"You're wrong about that. God gave you the ability to play a brass instrument, one that is challenging to learn, having only three valves to push. Or maybe the trombone is harder as it has no buttons at all," she mused.

"They're both difficult to play but for different reasons," Brandon said. "The trumpet embouchure is smaller than the trombone. Some find they need more strength to blow through it. The trombone, on the other hand … Oh, who cares? Certainly not me!"

So much for trying to get him off the pity path. "You don't strike me as the type to give up so easily," she said.

"It's called being realistic!"

"More like closed-minded!" she retorted. "Yes, you played the trumpet, having mastered the notes and octaves. But God gave you much more than your ability to perform in front of live audiences. You've been deaf and blind to anything else as you're stuck on what you can't do!

"Brandon, you have an auditory ability to hear pitch accuracy. You can read patterns on a music sheet. You've developed skills in time management and organization. You know what the critical elements of teamwork are, and you've found coping mechanisms to conquer fears like failure and stage fright. All these abilities can be transferred to a new career - songwriter, band manager, teacher, or motivational coach, to name a few. You can adapt."

"I don't want to! Being a trumpeter was my dream job. Nothing will ever top it."

"Okay. What about a prosthesis? Have you asked the docs about that?"

"I'll get fitted with something once the stump heals, but I can't play my trumpet using an appendage. Even if it were possible, which it isn't, no one is going to hire me over 'normal' people," he said, air-quoting with his right-hand fingers.

"Then what about…"

"Give it a rest, would you? You're not a counsellor; you're a high school kid!"

Casey opened her mouth, then closed it. She had all kinds of things she wished to say but remained silent as she pretended to be preoccupied with examining her nails.

"Did you bring my book?" Brandon asked in a milder tone. Without looking up, she replied no, that she hadn't touched it since the day he'd caught her standing at his bedside. "Oh," he said, looking puzzled. "I had assumed you borrowed it as it didn't arrive with the rest of my personal effects. It can't be lost; I've got to find it!"

"I'll re-check your room. If it's there, I'll have someone bring it to you," Casey said flatly.

"Not someone. You. With or without the book, you're to come tomorrow with your algebra textbook, seeing that you brought the down-payment with you." He reached for the sticky, chocolaty square, holding onto a piece of the plastic wrap with his teeth while his good hand removed the wrapping from around it. "Say hello to your father. Maybe he'd like to visit me?"

Her cue to leave. "I'm sure he would if he doesn't have to sneak his way in."

"Point taken. I'll add you both to the list."

She left knowing they'd be the only names on that list. Hopefully, in the not-too-distant future, his parents and friends would be added. A conversation she'd raise another day.

By the time Casey had returned to the farmhouse, she had bounced back from Brandon's rebuke. She immediately went to her room and sat behind her desk. Pressing the power button on her laptop, she impatiently waited for the log-in screen to appear. Several minutes later, she was Googling Brandon's name. She learned he wasn't in a band, at least not the kind she had envisioned. He'd been employed with an orchestra in Quebec and recently signed on with Hawkview's Symphony Orchestra as their principal trumpet player, the youngest to take on this position. "No wonder he's devastated," she muttered aloud. "A career about to take off then abruptly crashing. Loss of limb and career; a double tragedy." Her fingers flew over the keyboard as she entered search queries into her default search engine. She was reading up on a particular prosthetic elbow when she was interrupted by a rap on her bedroom door.

"What is it, Aaron?"

He apathetically walked to her bed, plunking himself onto it. "I don't think I should come with you to visit Dad this weekend."

Casey closed the lid of her laptop. "Why's that?"

"I don't always know what to say. And I'm afraid I'm going to say something dumb, like when I asked Dad how he tied his shoes with one hand."

"Did he answer you?"

"Sort of. He pointed to his running shoes. That's when I noticed the Velcro™ straps. Then he changed the subject, asking me about school, sports, and stuff."

"Your question was a fair one to ask, Aaron. You shouldn't feel guilty about it. How did Dad take your question? Was he upset?"

"No, he seemed matter-of-fact about it."

"That's great as he didn't express frustration. Dad is having to relearn things and find ways around every obstacle he faces. Tying his shoes is a prime example. When he changed the subject, he was deflecting the focus off his illness and the problems associated with it."

"I see. Dad wanted a distraction."

"Not just any distraction. Something of interest to him." Casey moved to the bed, sitting cross-legged beside Aaron. "When you were cooped up in your bedroom with strep throat, do you recall what you wanted from us?"

Aaron thought about it for a bit. It was back in February. Snow remained on the ground, and the cold north wind howled through the trees. And he had been bored stiff. "I wanted Harley in my room, which Dad said 'no' to."

"You used the poor-sick-me ploy hoping to get Dad to relent."

"I was sick, really sick, not that it seemed to make a difference with him," he said with mocked sadness.

"You knew that battle to be lost from the outset. What else?"

His eyes glazed over as he returned to that moment in time. It was calving season. With that realization, the memories rushed back. "Cocoa. I wanted to know if she had delivered her calf."

"And?"

"She did, but Dad said Cocoa refused to nurse her. I asked him why. He thought it was because she hadn't bonded to her newborn, the calf being her first one and because he had to assist with the birthing. Oh, and something about her hormone levels being out of balance."

"What else did you want to know about the calf?"

Aaron frowned. "I remember being worried about her. Wait, I know! I wanted to know if she accepted the bottle of colostrum. Jason said she took immediately to it!"

"When you asked those questions, it showed your desire to be connected to a world outside your bedroom walls. Dad wants one that's outside his hospital room."

"Doesn't he get that from watching the news?"

"The news doesn't tell him what's happening on the home front. He wants to hear about his family and the community he lives in."

Aaron perked up. "I can be his eyes and ears!"

"Don't be telling him everything," Casey said, wide-eyed. They both broke out laughing as they recalled the smoke from this morning's burnt toast, followed by a screeching alarm. On a more sombre note, she said, "Don't tell him of the problems we've been experiencing as we don't want to add anything else onto his plate. His priority should be on his recovery."

"I can keep secrets," he assured her.

The following day, Casey drove directly from her school to the hospital. Jason had offered to take Aaron to his basketball game, and he would stay to watch him play. The evening sun had not yet cast its shadows, yet inside her father's hospital room, it looked and felt gloomy. He was fully dressed, lying on his bed, staring up at the ceiling. His 'hi' was less than enthusiastic.

"How's your therapy been going?" Casey asked, angling her chair to face her father, only he wouldn't look at her.

"Which one, physio or speech? Actually, it doesn't matter as I'm doing the same at both. Lots of effort, little progress."

"It's only been a week when you said you'd give a more concerted effort. You can't expect dramatic changes to happen so quickly."

"Can't I? Isn't that what Jesus asks of us, to pray for our needs? We're to expect our prayers to produce results."

Casey was both confused and concerned. "Dad? What's going on?"

"Nothing!" he said as he got off his bed. He grabbed his quad cane and began pacing the room. "And that's the crux of the matter. I still drool and slur because I haven't adequate control of my mouth muscles. My hand remains weak. And this thing," lifting his cane, "remains my third leg. It's incredibly disheartening!"

Casey had never seen her father so exasperated. "I was recently reminded of what defines a person," she began. "It's not about what we don't have; it's all about what we do have. Jesus sees it that way too. He looks at one's heart and soul, at the fruit of the Spirit: 'love, joy, peace, patience, kindness, goodness, faithfulness, gentleness, self-control.'" (Galatians 5:22-23 NIV)

Jeffrey had stopped pacing and was leaning on Brandon's former bed for support. He was quiet for so long that Casey wondered if she'd been out-of-line. Perhaps he felt she was unsympathetic to what he'd been enduring. Maybe she should have allowed him to continue to vent.

His shoulders sagged as he spoke. "The pit of negativity is an easy one to fall into. One of the ways out is having an attitude of gratitude. Despite knowing that, I'm doing the exact opposite by complaining, criticizing, and being apathetic. It's an ongoing struggle," he confessed, "but one I need to overcome."

Casey sprung off her chair to wrap her arms around him. "I wish there were some way I could help you," she whispered.

Jeffrey returned the embrace. "You have, child. Thank you." He pulled back, tenderly stroking her face with the back of his hand. "You and the boys continue to be a blessing to me, especially during my recovery. Now go and check in on Brandon."

Casey pecked her father's cheek. "Love you, Dad." She picked up her backpack, slipping her arms through the straps and positioning them comfortably over her shoulders. She headed to the elevator. Once inside, she caught sight of a familiar object on the custodian's cart. Yours?" she asked, lifting the book. The custodian shook his head. "Then you won't mind if I take it as I believe I know who it belongs to." She received a shrug in response. "I'll need some of these," she said as she pulled disinfectant sheets from a container. Once off the elevator she settled into a visitor chair to wipe down the book.

"What are you reading?"

Casey looked up to find Caleb towering over her. "I'm not reading. I'm cleaning. The book belongs to Brandon," she replied as she began sterilizing the back cover. "It's been on an extended tour of the hospital." She gave a chortle at Caleb's baffled look. "I found it on a custodian's cart."

"May I?" Caleb asked, extending his hand. "Interesting title. Huh, not what I expected," he said as he leafed through the pages. He stopped at a photograph of arrowheads, scrapers, and other stone tools. Sitting down beside her, he showed her the picture. "Did you know that by hammering off the flakes from a lithic core stone, people in prehistoric times were able to make tools of various shapes and sizes? Stones were as precious back then as they are today. They've always had an important role to play. They're gems, in the real and figurative sense. Gemstones." He rose, handing her back the book before he took his leave.

Casey was perplexed by his remarks. By the time she had finished wiping down the book, she was no closer to understanding the relevance behind his gemstone comment. She concluded he was merely sharing his archaeology knowledge. Having tossed the disinfectant sheets into a trashcan, she made her way to the medical unit.

"The lost has been found," Casey proudly announced as she strolled into the room, holding up the book.

Brandon was depositing his toiletry bag onto the wardrobe's shelf. "I don't believe it!" he said, rushing around his bed to accept the book. Handling it as if it were a priceless item, he opened its cover and pointed to the inscription. "The author signed this one."

She came closer to view the signature. "But it's not dedicated to you," she said, confused.

"No, it's dedicated to my parents. They had gifted it to me. It was one of those lean years when they couldn't afford to buy me anything for Christmas."

"A gift of immeasurable value," said Casey. "And it keeps them close to you."

"It does."

"Then, why aren't they here?"

"My parents? I don't want them to know what's happened! I'll tell them once I've recovered."

"You haven't told them anything, not even about the accident?" Casey asked, stunned at this revelation.

"Don't you go lecturing me, too! I've had it with everyone advising me on what I should do. I've got the right to make my own decisions."

"Okay. Fine. I'll drop the subject."

"Thank you!"

A split second later, Casey crossed her arms. "No, I can't let this go. You've gone through several traumatic events - the accident, the first amputation, the infection, and then a further amputation. It's ridiculous that you haven't spoken to them about any of it! They're your parents! You've got to call them!"

Brandon's temper dissolved into laughter. "You should dye your hair auburn to go with those fiery eyes."

Casey blushed. "Sorry. I need to learn to control my outbursts." Tucking her hands into the front pockets of her blue jeans, she asked, with genuine concern, why he was avoiding his parents.

Brandon ran his fingers through his hair. "Look, I can barely handle my own emotions. I won't be able to handle theirs, too. Mom will be devastated. Dad, too, of course. And they'll pressure me to come home, but the Island isn't home anymore. It is, but it isn't. It's hard to explain."

"I think I know what you mean. The Island is where your parents live and where your childhood and youth memories originate from, but it holds nothing more as you've come to appreciate what city life has to offer. You're a city boy, no longer a country boy."

"Exactly."

"You also want to shield your parents from the emotional

turmoil that you've been experiencing. Feelings of sadness, worry, and grief."

"That's right. You do understand!"

She shook her head. "I understand, but I absolutely disagree with your decision."

"You think this is easy for me?" Brandon lashed out. "To go through this alone?"

"Who, in their right mind, chooses to go through a crisis alone?" Casey shot back. "You sure are one obstinate human being! Maybe you should get off your high horse and think of someone else's feelings besides your own!"

"I am! I'm thinking of my parents!" he said, glaring at her. "You know what else I'm thinking? That you should leave!"

Silence ensued as each stood staring intensely at the other. Casey relaxed her facial muscles and posture before speaking again. "Hey, I get that you love your parents and why you've put up the walls to protect them. The walls go up when you're faced with adversity. You take them down when you're sharing joys and successes. What you've done, in essence, is compartmentalized love. But that's not love, Brandon. Love is fluid, and it needs to be shared. It's what gives value to our successes and pulls us through difficult times.

"Do you think my dad wanted his children to witness his physical, emotional, and even spiritual struggles? I can't imagine how heart-wrenching it must be for him to have his weakness constantly exposed. But he doesn't exclude us. He includes us! We're part of his recovery team. Together, we journey through the gamut of emotions. Together, we problem solve, pray, and encourage. Love is what binds us together."

Brandon walked to his bedroom window, dropping his head against the pane. "They'll be overly worried and heartbroken," he finally said. "And angry."

"Normal reactions, don't you think?"

"I wouldn't know where to begin," he whispered.

"Does it matter? The key is starting the conversation, which means you need to call them."

Brandon turned around and looked at the phone that lay on his bed. "I'll think about what you've said. I'm not going to make any promises, though." Knowing it to be a step in the right direction, Casey decided not to push the matter any further, at least not today. "No more preaching from you," he said as he moved away from the window. "Time for me to take on the teacher role. Bring out your algebra textbook."

A couple of weeks later, Caleb caught sight of Jeffrey entering the therapy room for his daily workout, the automatic doors slowly closing behind him. He gave a wave from across the room when their eyes connected. His patient gave a brief nod in response. What was going on with him, Caleb wondered. He returned to the task of instructing Haley, his teenage patient, on the proper use of the pulley while keeping a watchful eye on Jeffrey, who remained at the door scanning the room.

Eventually, Jeffrey dragged his uncooperative right leg the short distance to a worktable, a place void of people. Plopping himself down on a chair, he shoved his cane beneath it. The tabletop held a large plastic tote overfilled with wooden blocks. He reached for it, grabbing hold of its side. With a quick jerk, he hauled it down. A loud crash ensued as wooden blocks sprayed across the table and onto the floor. "Sorry," he simply said as he swung his arm above his head to the unseen eyes staring at his back.

Another PT took steps in Jeffrey's direction, but Caleb signalled for her to stop. Jeffrey needed space, not help, not pity, and definitely not confrontation.

"Good job," praised Caleb to Haley, who worked the pulleys.

"Remember to keep your arm straight. You'll start to feel some strain in your shoulder, and that's okay. Hold it for the count of ten." Caleb briefly looked over his patient's shoulder at Jeffrey, who was pushing the blocks around. Not a particularly challenging exercise, to say the least. "You're doing great, Haley." He had her complete one more set. "Tomorrow, I want you to do the same - three sets of ten. Terrific effort," he said, patting her uninjured shoulder. Caleb had a brief word with his co-worker, who readily agreed to take on his other patient's care so he could give Jeffrey his undivided attention.

"Hey, that's cheating," Caleb jokingly said as Jeffrey used his left hand to negotiate blocks into their colour-specific row. "I'm going to have to tie your good hand behind your back if you keep favouring it."

"I appreciate all that you and your team have done for me, but I don't see the point of coming here anymore," Jeffrey replied, as he begrudgingly used his weak hand to manipulate the pieces. "I've made all the gains I'm going to make. I've reached my new normal, and I'm willing to concede to that. It's time we talk about discharge."

Caleb didn't reply to any of his statements. "These exercises are not only working on your hand dexterity but also on your mind," he said, picking up a coloured building block and stacking it on top of another. Jeffrey watched as several mini-towers were built on the table. "I want you to think of your brain as a metropolitan city; you'll be amazed at the similarities. Everything is interconnected by way of main roads, side roads, bridges, and tunnels," he explained as he built the city with blocks of different shapes, sizes, and colours. "It's a bustling place, a city that never sleeps. Much goes on to keep it operating at peak efficiency, day and night, without you even knowing about it."

Caleb picked up a block from the green tower he'd created.

"A city needs money to keep it operating, investments flowing in to keep it alive. If there's no economy, the city dies. The same goes for the brain. It needs food and stimulus to keep the brain active; otherwise, it dies."

Caleb gathered a coloured block from each of the towers he'd built, holding them up one at a time as he described their purpose. He began with the black block: "Think of this as the telecommunication hub that hears, sees, and reports on all things going on." Next was the purple block: "Legal department, to sort out what's right from wrong." Orange block: "University, for continual learning." Yellow block: "Transportation department, to keep things moving." Blue block: "Storage building. Think of it as the cache or RAM in a computer's hard drive where all the data is stored." Pink block: "Arts building, where creative ideas are generated." Jeffrey reached for a brown block, rolling the tips between his fingers. Caleb suddenly laughed. "Sanitation department," he said, taking hold of the block and placing it down in an empty spot.

Caleb tapped his forehead. "Our brain is like this colourful mess; everything in it is both independent yet connected. Independent, as it serves a specific purpose. Connected, because it can't work alone. All the pieces in our brain work according to God's design."

Jeffrey's eyes flashed at Caleb. "What did you say?"

"You heard me. It's not as if you hide the fact that you're a Christ-follower." Jeffrey shrugged in response.

Caleb pointed to the remaining towers. "As you can see, there are other departments that exist. We may not know their purpose, but we know there is one because God created an extremely complicated brain. While you're contemplating this wonderful city-brain analogy, you're probably asking yourself what the relevance of all this is to you."

"Oh, I know what you're getting at," Jeffrey said, toppling the orange tower with one swift shove. "God's perfect design has become permanently flawed."

"Has it?" Caleb placidly asked. "When an office tower is engulfed in a raging inferno, fire and rescue services are called to the scene. The teams do their utmost to salvage what they can. Once the fire is extinguished, an insurance adjuster visits the site to assess the damage. What happens next?"

"I don't know. You tell me," Jeffrey blandly replied.

"Oh, come on. Humour me."

"Fine. They rebuild."

"Exactly! Sometimes the rebuilding starts immediately, or it could be months down the road. Will the orange-university tower be built to the exact specifications as the original build? Highly unlikely, for various reasons. In this instance, there's a shortage of funds." He re-built the orange tower; however, it was smaller than the previous version. "This university is no longer capable of doing everything it once did, but all is not lost." Caleb began to add orange blocks to other coloured towers, making them wider or taller. "As I said earlier, a city's key buildings are interdependent on one another. If a tower goes down, they'll try to rebuild it as close to its former self as possible. If that's not possible, they'll remodel others to take on the additional responsibilities."

Jeffrey's forehead creased. With his left elbow resting on the table and his open palm supporting his head, his eyes surveyed the table. They travelled to the new orange-university tower and all the places the orange blocks were now a part of. "Are you suggesting that other parts of my brain will restore my losses?"

"Yes! It's possible as our brains have plasticity. Ha! Did you get that? PlastiCITY?"

"I got it," came the humourless response.

Caleb playfully smiled as he continued his wordplay. "Brain plasticity, neuroplasticity, neuroelasticity, or whatever city it's called, means the brain has the capacity to adapt. Our brains are not hard-wired; they can be rewired. Our brains can change. Your brain can change! Jeffrey, I don't believe this to be your new normal, and you shouldn't either. There are all kinds of rehabilitation techniques we can utilize to improve your functioning."

Jeffrey moved his tired right arm off the table to rest on his lap. "Okay. Let's just pretend that I believe you. How long are we looking at as I can't expect my kids to carry my burdens indefinitely? I'm supposed to be at home, managing the day-to-day operations of the farm. It's my responsibility to get Aaron to his games, buy the groceries, and pay the bills. I'm the parent. Not Casey. Not Jason. Me!"

"Jeffrey, as I just pointed out, our brains are complicated. I may not be able to tell you how long, but I can tell you that progress requires effort. This past week, it appeared you had succumbed to your stroke; your stroke was no longer your enemy but your friend. Your efforts at rehab became half-hearted again. Your soul appeared lost to despair and self-pity. But a few seconds ago, I heard anger. It came out raw, and it was genuine. Anger can be a healthy emotion. It forces one to fight back, and it's a powerful motivator. Channel your anger into effort!"

Jeffrey lifted an orange block, adding it to the stack. "That's it," Caleb said. "Start building skyscrapers, rather than knocking them down. Retrain your brain before it becomes hard-wired into the stroke way of doing things. Don't stop at the first sign of discomfort – push a little harder, a bit further.

"Do you want to be understood when you speak?" Caleb's eyes shone in response to Jeffrey's solid yes. "Good. Then practice your speech therapy exercises, no matter how lame you think they are! Casey is graduating in a few weeks. Don't you want to be home to celebrate with your family?"

Jeffrey sat straighter in his chair. "Of course I do." He hadn't noticed how quiet the room had become. A glance around showed everyone had left. "Is your shift over, or can you work with me a little longer?"

"If you're game, so am I. But first, I need to get something." Heading into the supply room, he exited, holding a bike glove.

"Only one?" asked Jeffrey, clearly confused.

Caleb slipped the glove onto his patient's left hand. "It's called conversion therapy. It's to remind you to use the weak one."

When Jeffrey returned to his hospital room, he found his daughter slumped in her chair, her head resting against the wall. Dr. Bleviss was right. His children were exhausted.

Casey awoke twenty minutes later, surprised to find her father in his wheelchair reading a novel. She massaged her neck and stretched her back. "Why didn't you wake me?"

"You appeared to need that power nap. Go home, Casey. I'm thankful for the time you kids spend with me, but I no longer need to be babysat or protected."

"That's not what we're doing," she insisted.

"No? Aaron brings me farm magazines and keeps me up-to-date on how his sports team is doing. What I didn't know was the number of practices and games he missed because there was no one to drive him. Jason insists we go outdoors during every visit for the fresh air, but I realize now that it was also for my mental health. He provides me with an abbreviated farm update leaving out crucial information like when the vet had to make an emergency visit to treat the sheep's hoof abscess. And you bring homemade meals to boost my appetite and provide me with general updates on what's been happening at home, church and with neighbours. But you've been holding back on me too. You picked up Old Digger's tractor part, the one I was to have picked up, only to find out that the wrong part had been shipped. You had to reorder it and reschedule the mechanic to repair it. Each of you skipped over concerns, feeding me only what you thought I should hear. And the blame falls squarely on me. I've become too self-centred."

"We thought if we shielded you from the problems at home, it would allow you to channel your time and energy into your recovery. Hey, how did you come to know about all those things?"

"You were sleeping so soundly that I didn't want to disturb you. I went and called Jason from the Quiet Room. I told him I wanted to know everything that was going on. Everything," he emphasized.

"Sounds like you're back to your old self."

"I feel like my heart, mind, and soul are once again in alignment. Go home, Casey. I don't want any of you visiting me until the weekend."

CHAPTER 5

"Tracked me down, did you?" Brandon said as Casey sat down in the recliner chair across from him. He had been writing in a workbook, which he let fall to his lap.

She pulled the handle located on the side of the recliner, releasing the footrest. Gently pushing on its arms, she tilted it back to a comfortable position. "They told me you had gone to the Quiet Room. What they neglected to tell me was on which floor."

"I come here for the comfy chairs. And the fact that hardly anyone is ever in here."

"What are you working on?" she asked. He lifted his Bible study journal. "I thought you didn't believe in God?"

"I never said that. Not exactly."

Casey thought back to the day when she had read to her father from the book of Philippians. "You insinuated it. You made disparaging comments. Clearly, you weren't interested in His word."

"Well, that was then. Things changed."

"What kind of things?"

"Oh, like your dad talking about the farmland he owns, calling it a gift even though it's full of rocks and hills, and this gratefulness list of his. He wouldn't let my … what did you call them, disparaging comments? He wouldn't let my disparaging comments pass without an explanation. He challenged me on my presumptions, and that forced me to dig deeper."

"Because you wanted a good rebuttal."

"Exactly."

"My dad isn't a debater."

"I know. I learned that quick enough! He throws questions back instead. Those "W" questions. What proof supports that notion? Where do you think that originated from? Why does culture behave like that? We've had some pretty good exchanges. He suggested I purchase a Bible study journal to write down my thoughts and questions as I read through scripture on my Bible app. He's a good teacher. I feel like I'm heading in the right direction."

Her eyes twinkled. "Sounds as if you've had a change of heart."

"It would seem so," Brandon grinned as he moved the journal from his lap to the floor. "How did you do with those questions I gave you?"

Casey moved her chair into the upright position. "I understood them all, except this one." An hour had passed when her phone's alarm buzzed. "Time for me to go."

"You can stay longer if you want," he offered.

"I can't. I promised Jason I'd be back early to help with the farm chores since Aaron is staying overnight at a classmate's home." Casey took hold of a strap on her backpack and slung it over her shoulder. "Thanks for the help. See you tomorrow."

The next day, inside the Physio Clinic, Caleb directed Jeffrey to take a seat on a nearby bench. "The team will be putting you through a series of tasks to evaluate your functional abilities. You did this when you were first admitted and then ten days later. We're going to evaluate your progress since that last assessment. Give it all you've got!"

For the next two hours, Caleb and his team assessed Jeffrey in the areas of mobility, communication, self-care, strength, and endurance. They observed his ability to sit, reach, zip, button, talk, lift, and a host of other tasks. As the team retreated to a nearby conference room to discuss his case, Jeffrey was left to wait on the bench.

When the door to the meeting room opened, Caleb's colleague requested Jeffrey join them. Once seated, Caleb had each health professional review the outcomes of their evaluation. At the conclusion, he thanked each for their input. "Jeffrey, you've heard from the team. What questions or comments do you have of us?"

"I can't think of any, for the moment. You've all been open and honest with where I'm at, which I truly appreciate. I hadn't realized all the gains I'd made."

"You've made excellent strides since our last review," confirmed Caleb. "As you've heard throughout the review, the potential remains for you to regain more of the functions you've lost. How much more and how long it will take is undetermined, but what we do know is that improvements continue to take place for up to a year post-stroke. We'll be recommending discharge, with the expectation that you continue treatment here, on an outpatient basis."

Jeffrey was elated with the discharge statement but not with the other. "That's not possible," he said to the group gathered around the table.

"What's not?" Caleb asked.

"Coming here as an outpatient. It's too long of a commute. Then there's the cost of gas and parking. What other options are there?" The group hashed out a plan to keep the therapy going from within his community. It included home exercises and visits to the local gym.

"We'd want you to return two weeks after discharge, and bi-annually after that, to monitor your progress," Caleb said.

"Sounds fair enough," Jeffrey replied. He then asked the question that had been on his mind throughout the meeting. "When, exactly, is my discharge date?"

"Dr. Hastings will let you know," Caleb said. "We'll be sending our recommendations and discharge plans to him."

The evening shift was coming on duty when Dr. Hastings and Dr. Bleviss entered Jeffrey's room. The book he'd been reading was bookmarked and closed as the doctors drew up chairs so as not to be hovering over him. "According to your team's report, you've done remarkably well," began Dr. Hastings. "They're recommending discharge, and Dr. Bleviss and I concur with their recommendation. However, first, we need to have services in place, such as Home Care."

"I can wait at home for that to happen," Jeffrey offered.

"Not ideal," said Dr. Hastings, "as the best discharges are planned discharges, where services and equipment are in place. There's safety equipment that needs to be picked up and installed, a tub grab bar and a raised toilet seat, for instance. We also want to discuss the discharge plan with your children as they play a key role in your wellness."

"And before you tell us that you don't want to burden your children," interrupted Dr. Bleviss, "know that they don't see it that way. Don't reject their offers of assistance. Be grateful instead. Quite frankly, you need them. Who else is going to remove those rugs in your house?" Jeffrey scrunched his face in puzzlement. "Tripping hazards," Dr. Bleviss pointed out. "They've got to go."

"With your permission," continued Dr. Hastings, "we'd like your children to be present at tomorrow's discharge meeting. The physiotherapist and speech therapist will review your home exercises, and our discharge nurse will review everything else. Any objections to bringing them in?"

"Aaron, too?" asked Jeffrey.

"Up to you," Dr. Bleviss said. "Casey and Jason should definitely be present."

"As for the discharge date," Dr. Hastings continued, "it's been scheduled for Thursday. I'll have your prescriptions ready for when you leave. You can pick them up on the way home. Any questions?"

"None that I can think of," said Jeffrey, itching to pull out his cell phone to share the news with his children.

Dr. Bleviss smiled widely. "Your children will be happy to have you back at home, as will your community."

Jeffrey knew him to be referring to their church community. After the doctors had left, he reflected on his absence from church life and how he missed being a part of it. He'd received visits from his pastor and congregant members, but what he longed for was corporate worship and serving. His ushering role would have to be put on hold; however, there were other positions he'd consider, such as door greeter or Sunday School teacher. Yes, he was looking forward to being back home.

Casey and Jason were mucking out the stalls when Casey felt the buzzing in the pocket of her overalls. She dropped her pitchfork into the wheelbarrow, recognizing the displayed number. "Hi, Dad," she answered. "Oh, wow. Home this Thursday? That is good news!" Jason came over from the pen he'd been working on to listen in. "Hold on, Dad. Jason's here, so I'm putting you on speakerphone. Okay, go ahead."

"I was saying that the hospital wants you both to come in

tomorrow to review what's needed in preparation for my return home. Drive the farm truck as they want you to pick up some equipment from the Red Cross' health equipment loan program." They chatted for a few minutes longer before disconnecting. Casey and Jason returned to their work, both lost in thought as they considered the positive and negative implications of his return home. Casey was the first to leave the barn, as she needed to start on supper.

An hour later, Jason hung up his coat inside the front door and headed down the hallway to wash up. He sat at the table just as Casey laid a steaming dish onto a homemade trivet. He prayed over their evening meal, acknowledging Jesus as their comforter and protector, asking forgiveness for sinful words and deeds, giving thanks that their father would soon be home and requesting he be restored to complete wellness. He ended with a blessing over their meal.

As the one-pot stroganoff dish was passed around, the threesome discussed their father's homecoming. Casey ladled the noodles-hamburger-mushroom mixture onto her plate. "After dinner, we should start removing the scatter rugs," she said.

"That shouldn't take long as there aren't that many," Jason said, reaching for a dinner bun from the breadbasket. He pulled it apart with his fingers as he listed the rugs' locations: entryway, hallway, and their father's bedroom. "We should probably remove the mats in the kitchen and bathroom as well."

Aaron accepted the ladle from Casey. "Don't forget the rug in the living room," he added as he dipped the spoon into the dish, filling it to overflowing.

"Right. The oriental rug. With all those furniture pieces holding it down, I think we can probably leave that one," Jason said. "The others can be stored in the spare bedroom."

Casey disagreed about the largest rug in the house. "The

under-padding lifts it off the floor by about a quarter-of-an-inch, which makes it unsafe. It has to go too."

"Okay, it'll be removed along with the others. What else did Dad say when he called?" asked Aaron. His brother filled him in about the scheduled meeting tomorrow. Jason then redirected the conversation inquiring about Aaron's next basketball game and the team they'd be playing. Casey joined in as she didn't wish to have their father's hospitalization overshadow every aspect of their lives. But it always did revert to him, which only confirmed how much they loved and missed him. "Maybe Dad can attend my next game."

"Let's first get him home," suggested Casey.

Not long after, Aaron was pushing back his chair. "I'm done. I'll start removing those rugs." His brother was quick to remind him that Harley had yet to be fed. Another reminder that things were not normal around their home as Aaron was not one to forget about his dog.

Aaron headed for the barn, whistling for his dog. He arrived from out of nowhere, panting hard. "What wildlife were you chasing this time?" he asked as he pulled open the barn door. Harley dashed to where his bowl laid and obediently sat by it as his master dumped dry food into it. When the "now" release command was given, he began crunching away at his meal. Aaron picked up the water bowl and left to re-fill it.

Meanwhile, Casey was in the kitchen, scraping dinner scraps off the plates and into the compost pail. As she deposited the dirty dishes into the dishwasher, Jason turned off the water tap, dunking a greasy frypan into the sink's sudsy hot water.

"Done!" Aaron exclaimed, grabbing hold of the door jam to fast-stop his sprint into the kitchen.

"That was quick," Jason said as he began scrubbing the frypan. "You can start removing the mats and rugs if you want, or …" He was gone.

Casey laughed. "Or wait for us? Was that what you were going to say?"

With kitchen clean-up completed, Casey and Jason entered the living room, where they found Aaron struggling to lift the leg of an armchair while simultaneously attempting to pull the rug from under it. Jason rushed over to lend a hand. What remained was the heavy, antique coffee table. Jason took hold of one end while Aaron and Casey held the other. Together they moved it onto the hardwood floor. The threesome then rolled up the large rug and awkwardly carried it into the spare bedroom.

"I'm going to call Dad," announced Aaron once the rug was dropped on top of the other displaced rugs and mats. As he left for his bedroom, Casey and Jason returned to the living room to restore the previously moved items to their original locations.

"Push it slightly my way," directed Casey, eyeing the coffee table to ensure it was centred in front of the couch. "Perfect!" She looked around the room to see what else remained to be done. "That's it. I'll make us some tea."

Jason restacked his father's books and magazines onto the coffee table. He tossed a fallen cushion onto the couch before following her to the kitchen. Leaning against the kitchen counter, he watched his sister scoop dry tea leaves from the ceramic container into the tea infuser. "Do you think we'll be able to manage Dad's care?" he asked. "I'm worried we might be taking on too much."

Casey flicked the electric kettle switch on. "Me too. I feel stretched to the limit as it is. I'm not sure how I'm going to get through exams next week, feeling as exhausted as I do." She poured the hot water into the teapot, watching the tea steep. "If they would only keep Dad until the following weekend, then we'd both be done with our exams. Should we ask?"

Jason opened an upper cupboard door to retrieve two mugs. "And disappoint Dad? No, we can't do that to him."

Picking up the teapot, Casey filled their cups. "A few weeks ago, we thought we were ready to have him home, but the doctors nixed the idea. It was a good thing that they did as we were nowhere near prepared. Now, he's got the green light to leave, but it's us that wants to postpone it."

"They won't keep him in the hospital if they feel he's ready to be discharged," stated Jason. "I guess we'll find out more tomorrow as to what Home Care can offer. Maybe our caregiving responsibilities won't be as much as we fear them to be."

The following day's discharge conversation brought forth a mixture of emotions: excitement because their father would soon rejoin the family at Rocky Meadows and disappointment at having learned what services Home Care would provide. There would be no nursing services as he didn't require any; however, he would receive a bath assist once a week.

Next came the exercise expectations. Caleb provided Casey with handouts and a calendar so she and Jason would know their father's schedule, routines, and which exercises required their assistance. A physiotherapist would come in once, possibly twice, to ensure Jeffrey continued to perform them with proper technique.

The speech therapist also provided exercise handouts, but neither Casey nor Jason was to be involved. "You are to practice in front of a mirror, Mr. Kallan, just as you've been doing here," she said. "What he'll need from you two is the encouragement to read aloud. The more he practices, the easier it'll come."

Jeffrey's children departed shortly after the team did, wanting to get on the road to pick up the required items before rush-hour traffic hit. "I wasn't quite sure what to expect," admitted Casey as Jason drove to the Red Cross building for the authorized list of equipment. "I didn't know Home Care couldn't help with making meals or cleaning the house. The things we needed help with, no one could provide."

"And transportation," chimed in Jason. "Why would we want to pay a driving service to take Dad to his appointments? We might as well do it ourselves."

Casey brought attention to the fact that it would result in further absences from school. "Let's keep open the driving service option if we can't find a volunteer to take him," she suggested. "In another month-and-a-half, Dad will receive an evaluation for driving. We'll pray he'll receive the medical clearance."

Inside the Red Cross building, Jason handed over the equipment referral form to the receptionist. As they waited for the items to arrive, they brainstormed how they could become more efficient with meals and household management. "We have freezer meals that the church members and neighbours prepared," Casey said. "We could make smaller portions for Dad to warm up for his lunch." They kept throwing out ideas as they carried the equipment to the truck.

Inside the Kallan home, Jason immediately went to work installing the raised toilet seat and the tub grab bar. Casey tended to the farm chores, and Aaron worked on his homework. It was midnight when Casey closed her schoolbooks. She slipped under her bedcovers and fell instantly asleep.

Early the next morning, Jeffrey was at the Physio Clinic, choosing a five-pound dumbbell from the stand. "You're late," he said, looking disapprovingly at Caleb as he entered the room. "I came at the prearranged time, but you weren't here. What happened?" he asked as he sat down on a bench to begin a set of reps with his right hand.

Caleb walked towards him. "Remember when I told you that I was renting a furnished condo?" Jeffrey nodded his head. "Well, this morning, a water pipe burst on the floor above me. There's significant damage, which means I can't stay in the place. I've been on the phone with the condo owner, and I've already packed and moved my personal effects into a motel. That's why I'm late."

"You've had quite the morning, and it's not even 8 a.m.," Jeffrey exclaimed as he completed another set of reps.

"It's not what I had envisioned for my holidays, which start next week."

"I forgot about that. What did you call it?" he asked while returning the weight to the dumbbell stand.

"A staycation. I can make it work," Caleb said in a less than convincing voice.

"Eating out for all your meals? Being cooped up in an oversized bedroom? I doubt you'll be happy there," Jeffrey said as he walked over to the pulleys. A light-bulb moment occurred to him. "You could stay with us! We've got the room. You'd have engaging company, and I've plenty of books you can read." He moved the peg on the weight stack to add additional kilograms. With his right hand, he took hold of the D-handle. "The invite comes with fresh air, wide-open spaces, roosters crowing at daybreak, coyotes howling at night, and a menagerie of animals, including a hyperactive Blue Heeler dog. How about it?"

Caleb watched his patient work the pulleys as he mulled over the offer of a farm vacation. "Okay, but on one condition," he said. "You have to accept my caregiving services as compensation for your hospitality." Jeffrey reluctantly agreed as Caleb would have it no other way. "I wish I could drive you home tomorrow to save Casey from having to make an extra trip in, but I've still Friday to work."

"Casey would come in regardless, to say goodbye to Brandon. I'm assuming you have a map app on your phone to find our rural address?" He confirmed that he did.

Jeffrey received a less-than-enthusiastic response from his daughter when he shared the latest news. "Caleb has offered to be my caregiver," he reminded her, "which will free up personal time for you and the boys."

She had been in her car waiting for Jason in the school parking lot when she took the call. When they had hung up, she revisited the conversation. "There's no such thing as free time when you have a houseguest," she voiced bitterly. She started a mental to-do list: more groceries to buy, removing the rugs from the spare room, clean sheets on the guest bed. Jason opened the passenger door, and one look at Casey told him something was amiss. He patiently listened as she vented her annoyance.

"Initially, it sounds like additional work, but I think Caleb will be a blessing, not a hindrance," Jason said. "Think about it. Dad will have an in-home physical therapist, he won't be alone when we're in classes, and he'll have someone to drive him to his appointments and the gym."

"Good points," she conceded. "You saw the upside to my downside. When we get home, we'll need to find a new home for those rugs in the spare room. Which location is better, crawl space or garage?"

"Neither. It'll be too difficult to get the oriental rug into the crawl space. In the garage, mice will move into their new homes. They'll likely make renovations so that their extended family can join them," he said, laughing. She could envision the damage gnawed holes and nest-building would cause. Jason offered to have the rugs stored temporarily in his room. "Once Caleb leaves, we can move them back into the spare room," he said.

"Or maybe Dad will have decided they need to be removed permanently," submitted Casey. "Anyway, if you're okay with them being relocated to your room, then that's where they're going." She turned the car into the junior high school's parking lot. Aaron was sitting on the grass in front of the school, talking animatedly with a bunch of his friends. She honked the horn to get his attention, but it was his friend's attention she caught. Aaron was jabbed in the shoulder as his friend pointed to the waiting vehicle. He scrambled to his feet, giving a hasty goodbye to the group.

The spare room transformation went a lot quicker than anticipated. The boys removed the rugs and mats while Casey changed the bedsheets, dusted, and brought fresh towels into the small ensuite. "Anything else?" Aaron asked.

"Not here," Casey said, taking a final glance around. "I did Dad's room yesterday. What remains is the laundry in the dryer. If you put that away, I'll start on supper, and Jason can tend to the animals. They parted to attend to their assigned tasks.

Casey left the house early Thursday morning so she could make Brandon her first visit. When she entered his room, she found him packing. "Moving back to the rehab wing?"

"I've been kicked out," he said, placing his folded clothes into the small suitcase. "I'll be booked in for a prosthetic fitting as an outpatient. And, in a couple of weeks, I should be out of this walking boot." He stopped packing when he saw her upset face. "What's the matter?"

"I might have walked into an empty room."

"Casey, I wouldn't have left without saying goodbye," he said, resuming his packing. "Your dad told me you'd be coming by this morning. Are you worried about your exam?"

"A little," she confessed, leaning her back against the wall.

He zipped the suitcase closed. "Well, don't be. You'll do fine." Removing his jacket from the closet, he pulled its sleeve over his stump then took hold of the collar to get it over his shoulder. "Are you going to miss me?" he asked as he wiggled his other arm into the sleeve.

"Yes. I've enjoyed having you as my tutor. We've become friends, haven't we?"

"We have. It was a bit of a rough start, but we got past that, or perhaps I should say that I got past it. Take out your phone," Brandon ordered. He rattled off his personal information for her to add to her contact list. He looked smugly at her. "I already have yours. Your Dad gave it to me when he dropped by my room last night."

"Are we interrupting?" asked the lady who had walked in on them.

"We were just saying our goodbyes. Mom, meet Casey, the young lady who's been prodding me these past few weeks."

Casey received a motherly hug. "We have you to thank, then. My son has a lot of pride, and like his dad, it often gets in the way of common sense."

Over his mother's shoulder, Casey mouthed: You called?

Brandon's eyes gleamed. He looked around his mom. "Where is Dad?"

"Parking the car. He should be here any minute."

"I'm here," came the voice from behind. "And who's this?" Brandon's father asked, smiling down on Casey. When Brandon made the introductions, her hands were immediately engulfed in his father's rugged ones. "We owe a debt of gratitude to you." He moved to the bed, lifting the suitcase off it. "Ready, son?"

"I'll be down in a few minutes." When his parents had left the room, Brandon told Casey that they'd be staying in town until the prosthetic fitting. "They're going to help pack up my place as I'll be returning with them to the Island. With no job, I have no reason to stay here. I'll have plenty of time to decide on my next career."

"I still think you can play your instrument. There are lots of musicians with disabilities that do."

Brandon laughed. "Forever the optimist. Fine. I'll ask some questions when I get my prosthesis. Will that meet with your approval?"

"Not quite. You need to ask for the names of companies in eastern Canada that can design and build a special one for you."

"Okay, okay. Anything else, counsellor?" he asked with a wry smile.

"You know me. I always have more to say. Actually, just one thing. Promise me you'll find a Bible study group to join."

Brandon raised three fingers. "Scouts honour. Can I give you a hug?" She nodded. "I'll miss you," he said as they embraced. Taking a step back, he added, "I'm not sure what state I'd have been in had your father and I never shared a room."

"Jesus may have orchestrated the opportunities for discussion, but you had to be a willing participant. Had you closed your heart …"

"… I'd still be lost and miserable. I'm grateful for the coaxing and support I received from you and your father," he said as he gathered the last of his personal effects. They walked off the unit together, riding the elevator to the ground floor. Stepping out of it, Brandon did a quick visual sweep to locate his parents. He spotted them standing by the entranceway. "Keep in touch," were his parting words as he left to join them. With mixed emotions, she exchanged final goodbye waves. Parents and son were soon out of sight. Reversing direction, she headed to the Rehab Unit.

Casey found her father at the nursing station signing his discharge papers. "Here's your prescription," the nurse said, handing him a slip, "and here's a reminder card with your follow-up appointment. We wish you the very best, Mr. Kallan."

On cue, a porter brought forth a wheelchair. "Why am I being wheeled out when I can walk?" he grumpily asked as he handed the porter his cane. Gripping the chair's sidearms, he lowered himself onto the vinyl seat.

Casey temporarily ignored the question as she set a box of chocolates on the counter along with a handmade thank-you card signed by each member of the Kallan family. She expressed gratitude to the nurse manager for the care her father received. They spoke a few more minutes before Casey turned to her father to reply to his question. "Hospital rules. Legal liability and such."

She lifted his suitcase, placing it on his lap. To the porter, she indicated that she'd take over. Unlocking the brakes, Casey pushed her father off the unit for the last time. Jeffrey clung onto the case with his right hand, waving goodbye to staff and patients with the other.

Standing in the entryway of their home, Jeffrey leaned on his four-prong cane and said: "She's right, you know." Casey set down his suitcase and asked who he was referring to. "Dorothy, from The Wizard of Oz, because she said, 'there's no place like home,' and she was right."

"There's no place like home without *you*," Casey said, hugging her father. "Why don't you go into the living room while I make us a pot of tea."

Jeffrey slowly made his way to his favourite chair. Once comfortably settled, he looked around the room. Everything was as before, but not quite. He was trying to figure out what it was when Casey entered, carrying a tray laden with a teapot, mugs, and a glass dish filled with vanilla wafer cookies. He was about to tell her to be careful when he realized what was different - the oriental rug was gone.

Casey poured the tea and handed him the steaming mug, tears welling up in her eyes.

"Honey, what's wrong?"

It was a familiar sight, him holding onto his mug of tea with his legs stretched out, crossed at the ankles. "Absolutely nothing," she said, beaming. "It's good to have you home, Dad!"

CHAPTER 6

Casey slowed down her car as she drove past Caleb and her father, walking down the lane to the Kallan home. Jason had been right; Caleb was a blessing relieving them of the very burdens they had feared. Together, he and her father tidied the house, did the dishes, and prepared the meals. Caleb made him read aloud everything to strengthen his mouth muscles, thereby improving his speech: Bible passages, novel pages, and even his mail. He purchased a portable mini exercise machine enabling her father to work both his hands and feet. A gift, Caleb had said, for the free room-and-board. And, he drove their father everywhere he needed to go. She hadn't felt this well rested in weeks. When Caleb wasn't attending to her father's needs, playing board games with the family, or tossing the football around with her brothers, he was going for long walks with Harley at his side. He turned out to be the perfect helper and the guest that lessened their burdens, not added to them.

Jeffrey and Caleb entered the house. "You're home early," her father noted.

Casey placed a plate of sweets on the coffee table. "We could leave as soon as we finished the exam," she said, slipping into the kitchen to retrieve the milk for Caleb's coffee. "It was my last one. No more studying! No more school!" she gleefully exclaimed as the men sat down.

"And?" her father asked, reaching for a butter tart. "How do you think you did?"

"I took Caleb's advice and started on the questions I did know, then focused on the harder ones. As for the algebra problems, I think I answered the polynomials correctly and the linear equations. I had difficulty with the exponential functions and some others. Overall, I'm hoping for at least a B grade."

"I'd probably fail them all," her father said, taking a bite of his pastry. "Polynomials? Exponential something or other? You should get marks for being able to pronounce the words, let alone understand them." Caleb and Casey looked at one another in amazement. "What?" asked Jeffrey suspiciously.

"Did you hear yourself?" asked Caleb. "You spoke those words clearly and distinctly."

"You did, Dad! Maybe you should start reading something else to practice your enunciation. I've got just the one for you." She left the room, returning with a paperback. He laughed a hearty laugh when she deposited a book on tongue-twisters on the table before him.

Dinner was a boisterous event. There was so much to celebrate with Casey's grade 12 exams over with and their father's speech returning to near normal. It's why she hadn't noticed when Aaron slipped out of the room, returning on a wave of applause as the chocolate layer cake with *Congratulations* spelled out in yellow icing was placed before her. He inserted a star-shaped sparkler into its centre and used a butane lighter to bring the sparkler to life. For the next few seconds, they watched as gold sparks spewed into the air and onto the cake.

"I'll get the dessert plates," volunteered Jason. It wasn't plates he brought back but gift-wrapped boxes which he set before his sister.

"What's this?" Casey asked,

"Your graduation gifts, silly," replied Aaron. "The cake was from Caleb. This one is from me," he said, handing her a rectangle box.

"Thank you, Caleb." She turned Aaron's gift over multiple times, trying to find a starting place to peel off the paper. "Jason, would you mind cutting and distributing the cake? It may take some time to open Aaron's gift as he super-taped it," she said, chuckling. He returned to the kitchen, this time bringing back dessert plates and forks. Casey reached for her steak knife, digging the tip into the tape to rip a hole through it. Not long after, she withdrew an object cushioned within the recycled filler. "Thanks, Aaron!" having unwrapped the Willow Tree Grateful Figurine®. She passed it around for all to admire. "It's beautiful!"

Next was Jason's gift. "I always wanted one of these," she said, reviewing all the items inside the emergency roadside vehicle kit.

"You can get rid of the cardboard box in your trunk, the one you store the jumper cables in," he said.

"I love the fact that you think of such practical gifts. Thank you."

The last gift was a leatherette jewellery box. She gently raised its lid, giving a sharp inhale of breath at what she beheld. "Mother's diamond pendant," she said as she lifted it with reverence off the velvet square.

"I had it cleaned and the clasp fixed," her father said. "She would have been so proud of you. We all are."

"Thank you for these treasures," she said with sincerity.

"Now can we eat cake?" Aaron asked, waving his fork.

"How about we take a moment to give thanks to Jesus," Jeffrey suggested. "Caleb, could I ask you to lead us in prayer?"

Caleb reached out to join hands with Jeffrey and Aaron. Casey and Jason joined hands to unite the circle. "Heavenly Father, we give thanks that you remain at the centre of this family's life, holding them tightly together. We thank you for providing Casey with the calmness required for her to write that challenging math exam. We ask that you reveal to her what the next chapter in her life is to be. She has many admirable qualities. Use them to bless others. We thank you for Jeffrey and the remarkable recovery he has made. We ask for the continued healing of his body. Thank you for Jason and Aaron. Continue to bless these young men as they walk in your way. Give them discerning minds and hearts that they may experience the fullness of your goodness. In Jesus' name, we pray. Amen."

Later that evening, Caleb caught Casey before she entered her bedroom. "I've got something for you," he said, holding out a small parcel. "It's from Brandon."

"How did you get this?" she inquired, accepting the package.

"I was milling about the hospital waiting for your dad to finish with an appointment when I spotted him in the gift shop. We chatted a bit, and before we went our separate ways, he asked if I'd hand-deliver it."

"Come in," she said, grabbing a pair of scissors from her desk drawer before sitting on the edge of her bed. "What's your take on how Brandon is doing?"

Caleb took possession of the desk chair and watched as she cut away the packing tape. "He's adjusting. Being inside Hawkview Hospital's walls provided him with a degree of emotional safety because of the empathy he received from medical staff, fellow amputees, a caring roommate, and the roommate's family. But when he's out and about, among the public, he admitted to feeling vulnerable and exposed."

"In time, and with God's help, he'll become more immune to those feelings," Casey predicted. "My prayer is that he'll learn to cope by staying involved in life, not by withdrawing from people."

"He assured me that he doesn't plan to retreat behind walls, or curtains, ever again having experienced first-hand what isolation and loneliness can do to one's psyche."

"Well, that's good to hear," she said as she flipped up the plastic lid of the gift box. "He sent me a text message stating he and his parents had arrived safely back home on Prince Edward Island. He's going to try farm life again, not as a field labourer but in the office managing payroll and business accounts. Brandon has truly re-engaged in life, hasn't he?"

Caleb nodded. "He certainly has. Perhaps he'll enrol in an accounting program if he finds himself enjoying this new line of work."

"I wouldn't be surprised if he did, knowing his love of numbers." In her heart, she hoped he would pursue his music career, if not as a trumpeter, then in an occupation that kept him in the music field. He was too gifted to throw away his talent. Casey lifted an object wrapped in tissue paper from the box. Carefully, she tore away the delicate paper revealing a thin, polished, iris agate rock nightlight. She picked up the box to retrieve the card tucked within it, silently reading the scribbled message: Something to remember me by, warmest regards, Brandon. She lightly laughed when she read the postscript: P.S. This stone does glow! Casey plugged in the nightlight, stepping back to observe the rainbow of colours that shone through it.

"Very nice," Caleb acknowledged while she returned to the bed, picking the card up once more. "Unusual kind of gift, though. It must have a special significance for you."

"Mm-hmm," she said, rereading her card. Caleb quietly retreated from the room.

A week had passed since her last day of classes. It was early morning; the sun had yet to rise. Casey was pouring her tea into a travel mug when Caleb entered the kitchen, greeting her as he headed to the cupboard for the jar of instant coffee.

"Why are you up so early?" she asked.

"Couldn't sleep," he replied as he added a heaping spoon of coffee powder into a mug. He felt the side of the kettle. Finding it to be hot, he poured the water over the coffee granules, stirring until they dissipated. "What's your excuse?"

"The rain."

"The rain? It's barely drizzling out. How can that keep you awake?"

"I didn't say it did." Casey reached for another travel mug from the shelf and placed it on the counter. "Finish making your coffee, then transfer it into this and follow me." Locating flashlights and retrieving a throw blanket from the hutch, she headed for the door.

"Where are we going?" Caleb inquired, lifting his coat off the hook and slipping it on.

"For a short hike. Hurry up, or we'll miss it!" she said, leaving the house with the blanket draped over her arm. Caleb closed the door and ran to catch up to her.

The morning air smelled clean and fresh from the recently fallen rain. It also meant having to walk on a muddy trail and sidestepping puddles. Soon they were trudging upward. On the hilltop, Casey briefly scanned the surroundings with her flashlight. She quickly found the path she needed to follow. They walked a short distance further, stopping at a fallen log. Here she laid down her blanket and invited Caleb to sit down beside her.

"And we're here because why?" he asked.

"Be patient. You'll know when you see it," Casey said, turning off the flashlight.

"Oh, so we're going to sit in the dark," Caleb stated, pocketing the flashlight he carried.

"It won't be for long," she promised. "See? The orange is rising on the horizon." They sat wordlessly, watching as rays of red and yellow blended in to paint the morning horizon. Without taking her gaze off the unfolding sunrise, Casey expressed her heartfelt gratitude to him for having gone beyond the regular caregiving duties. "You've been a blessing to us all. Dad has certainly improved, and credit must go to you for your persistence in keeping him engaged and motivated."

"Your father is a remarkable man."

"Isn't he, though? He's endured a lot in his life, like his parents, brother, and wife's deaths and having to raise the three of us on his own. Then there's the stroke and his recovery. But he rarely complains, and he doesn't get upset without cause."

"Like when he wanted to give up prematurely?" teased Caleb.

"He was frustrated, impatient, and annoyed with himself for the things he couldn't do. There was an element of fear there, too, of not improving. Guilt played a huge role."

"Typical and expected human emotions," Caleb summarized. "And ones that he was able to work through. I've enjoyed spending time with your father. We've had some rather interesting discussions. I'm impressed with his biblical knowledge and interpretation."

Casey suddenly grabbed Caleb's arm. "Look!" As the early morning rays touched the wet landscape, everything glistened - stones, blades of grass, and leaves.

"Beautiful," replied Caleb, mesmerized by the scene. "Gemstones, gem-grass, gem leaves."

"Gemstones I see, but gem-grass and gem-leaves? They're not even words."

"Everything God has made He considers precious. He created it all. You know the Bible verse about the sparrows in Matthew 10:29-31: 'Are not two sparrows sold for a penny? Yet not one of them will fall to the ground outside your Father's care. And even the very hairs of your head are all numbered. So don't be afraid; you are worth more than many sparrows.'" (NIV)

Casey liked where he was going with this. "Gem-sparrows, gem-trees, gem-flowers."

"Exactly." Caleb turned to face Casey. She turned half her face towards him as she didn't want to miss the evolving spectacle. "And the most valuable of all things He created? Gem-mankind. And you, Cassandra Claire Kallan, are very precious in God's sight."

That got Casey's undivided attention as she immediately stood up, anger flashing from her eyes. "How dare you presume to know God's will! I am no more precious than you are, or anyone else for that matter!"

Caleb calmly replied: "Did I not just quote a bible verse stating mankind is more valuable than many sparrows? Mankind is the most precious gem of all, and that includes you." He rose to stand face-to-face with her. "And yes, you are much more precious than I, for I am God's representative, an angel, sent for a purpose."

Casey's eyes narrowed as she took a hesitant step backwards. No way, she thought, and yet, she knew it could well be true. Was she being conned, or was she indeed in the presence of a heavenly host? How was she to know for sure? More questions surfaced in her mind as she watched Caleb stretch his hand over the ground. Her eyes widened, her jaw dropped as dazzling colours danced at their feet. It was breathtaking. It was incredible. It was impossible! When he closed his hand, it all disappeared.

Caleb chuckled lightly. "Without the proverbial wings, what proof did you have that I am who I said I am?"

"An angel!" she declared in stunned disbelief. "I've been living with an angel!" Then a previous comment of his came to mind. "You said you came for a purpose. What purpose?"

"Initially, it was to help your father. He had prayed for healing, and God knew the healing that needed to take place was not his body but his soul. Then, when I prayed at the supper meal for the next chapter in your life to be revealed, He gave me a new assignment. You.

"Come, sit down, and I'll tell you what He asks of you." Caleb pulled on her hand when she showed ambivalence to sit beside him. "There's a lot of troubled people in this world. They're like gems that have lost their lustre; God wants you to help them."

"He wants me to make them feel better, to polish them up and shine?" she asked.

"Sort of, but not quite. Polishing only makes the outside shine. It's superficial. God wants you to help them shine from the inside out."

"Well, He's chosen the wrong person. I've only just finished high school! I'm average. And clearly, I'm no therapist!"

"That's not what you've recently shown Him."

"What are you talking about?"

"Remember the 'Stone' word that radiated off the cover of Brandon's book?"

"You knew about that? Of course you did," Casey snorted.

"Brandon was the gem that needed shining. He thought he'd lost his purpose in life because of the amputation. You helped him see past it by simply accepting him the way he was, physically incomplete yet fully complete. He'd not only lost himself, but he was in danger of losing his family, and what was even more concerning was that he'd lost his way from seeing Jesus."

"A lot of that was Dad's doing," noted Casey. "He's the one who spent time going deeper with Brandon, not me."

"That's true," conceded Caleb. "But your father was the waterer. You were the planter. You planted seeds of hope and possibilities. And they took root." Caleb took hold of her hands. "Casey, God has chosen you. He doesn't make mistakes. There are no superheroes in the Bible, only ordinary people who did extraordinary things because of their belief."

She thought back to an earlier conversation. "It's not about being average; it's about using my natural talents and spiritual gifts."

"You're such a quick study."

That made her laugh. "Okay, I'm in. Tell me more."

Caleb released her hands. "There are three things you need to know and remember. Number one," he said, raising his thumb, "God's chosen person will be identified to you by a stone. Two: God will give you the skillset required for the assignment. Three: you are never alone. The Holy Spirit is always with you, as is God your Father, Jesus your Lord and Saviour, and your earthly father, a lovely, righteous man."

"Let me make sure I heard you correctly," Casey said. "God is going to show me the person I'm to help by way of a stone?"

"Correct. But don't assume it to be a physical stone. It could be a name, place, idea, or thing."

"Like the book's title."

"Like the book's title," repeated Caleb.

"Why's He making it so mysterious? Why not whisper it in my ear or something?"

"You want me to question His motives? Rest assured that the chosen client will be made obvious to you, and only you."

Casey recalled the book's title. That certainly was obvious enough. "And these skill sets I'm to receive, are they temporary or permanent?"

"Temporary."

"Temporary skills. Why would that be?" Casey asked. "Is it because my roles are temporary?" Caleb nodded. "What kind of roles are we talking about?"

He shrugged. "I've no idea."

"And where do I find these clients?"

"You're going to like this," Caleb said, pulling out a small business card case from his pocket and handing it to her.

She withdrew a card, reading the business name aloud. "Kallan Temporary Staffing Solutions."

"You're the sole proprietor and sole employee."

"I'm the temporary staff," Casey paraphrased.

"Right! Oh, and you'll need this," handing her a cell phone. "It's assigned to the number on your business card. And no, you don't get an office, in case you were wondering."

Casey felt overwhelmed. Her own business, a work phone, and business cards. And she'd be working for God! She stared at the phone and business card case she held. Doubts started creeping in. "What if I'm not successful?"

"Then, perhaps His client wasn't ready or willing to accept the help."

"But what if I'm not ready?" she anxiously asked.

"Casey. You're not alone in this, remember?"

"Does anyone else know? About you?"

"No, to both questions. You, however, can share our conversation with your father."

"What about my brothers? Can I tell them?"

"You can tell anyone on a need-to-know basis."

"So, what you're saying is that I'm not to tell people unless I absolutely need to."

"Do you want it to be about you?" Caleb asked.

"Of course not!" she fired back. "Why would you even suggest that?"

"You tell me."

Casey pondered the question at length. Why would it matter if she shared with her family or with her clients that she was on assignment for God? How would her family react? Wouldn't clients be inspired to work towards positive change if they knew? Would they be envious or skeptical? She seemed to have more questions than answers. And what answers she did come up with converged to the same point. "It would be about me," she said, sighing. "My brothers would treat me differently. Not intentionally, but the dynamics would change because they'd know. And should they let it slip to others, repercussions could be far-reaching. As for my clients, there's a strong possibility that they wouldn't work on resolving their issues. They'd likely expect a miracle directly from God to fix them or from God through me to them. On the flip side, clients might turn their backs on me. Believers would want proof. Unbelievers would label me a nut case."

This girl is wise, thought Caleb. "Very good. You do see the bigger picture. That's why you need to exercise caution whenever you are considering revealing details to others. Weigh the pros and cons, as revelations can undermine the work you are trying to achieve. Now, the answer to your unspoken question of when? Anytime."

Casey tried to show a stoic face as guilt feelings welled up inside. Her siblings would again have to take on additional household and farm responsibilities during her absences. How could she leave her father? He hadn't fully recovered from his stroke impairments. Perhaps she could start after he was better. But, she knew it wouldn't end there as other excuses would emerge. There was only one response to being called. It wasn't 'no' or 'wait'; it was 'yes.' Casey looked assuredly at Caleb. "I'll go when and wherever God tells me."

"Your father is getting stronger with each day." Without turning around, Caleb said, "Look behind you and see for yourself."

Casey turned to find her father walking towards them using his quad cane. "Dad!" she joyously yelled. She ran to him, amazed he had walked such a distance on his own. "I'm so glad to see you! I've got so much to tell you!"

As they embraced, Jeffrey wondered for the umpteenth time why Caleb had requested he meet him here, at this exact time. There had been no explanation, only a request that he be punctual. When he had topped the summit of the small hill, he had spotted his daughter, seemingly in a serious conversation with Caleb. Why this clandestine meeting? Casey had turned around as if she had heard his thoughts. Her face initially showed surprise and then delight. From that reaction, it was clear she had not been expecting him.

Casey let spill all that had transpired. Jeffrey listened in awe. "Incredible, right?"

Jeffrey briefly studied the business card he'd been handed. "I'm both humbled and overwhelmed, Caleb, that God should choose this child, my child, for such a task."

"God loves his children," declared Caleb. "All his children." Jeffrey smiled in acknowledgment. "You've come a very long way in your recovery."

Casey's eyes widened. "Caleb. You're leaving us." It was a statement, not a question.

"I am."

"How soon?" she asked.

"My work here is done, Casey. There's no need for me to remain."

"Will we ever see you again?" she asked.

Caleb handed her his flashlight. "Honestly, I don't know."

He turned to walk the path now visible by dawn's light. Father and daughter watched, each having linked an arm around the waist of the other.

Suddenly, Caleb stopped and made an about-turn. He swept his arm in an arc. "This land is full of gems," he said. "You need to dig a little deeper."

Jeffrey and Casey looked at one another, perplexed by this strange statement. "What do you mean by …" began Jeffrey, but his words hung in the air as Caleb had vanished.

Father and daughter slowly made their way down the hillside to home. It was trickier going down the wet terrain than it was going up. "What do you think he meant?" asked Casey.

Jeffrey chuckled. "It's likely metaphorical as there's no mineral vein lying in these lands."

Several days had passed since Caleb had left the Kallan family. The boys were initially upset that he hadn't said goodbye to them, but then the email arrived in their inbox. Caleb had written to them both, but neither revealed its content. All they said was that he apologized for having to leave so abruptly and how much he had enjoyed his time with them.

Today, Casey was relaxing in her father's lawn chair, the one at the back of the house. With her Bible on her lap and her eyes closed, she inhaled the fragrant scent of the roses that wafted from the rose garden. When friends had learned what precipitated Jeffrey's stroke, they came together to plow and plant the garden. Each had contributed a colourful, hardy rose plant, and the Kallan children purchased and planted their father's favourite - the Morden Centennial Shrub Rose.

Caleb's final words lingered on Casey's mind. She refused to believe them to be figurative; he was telling them something. She got up to find her father, locating him in his office, reviewing the farm accounts. She rapped on the open door. "Can I come in?"

"Certainly," Jeffrey said, removing his glasses and setting them on the desk. "What's on your mind?"

"I've been giving some thought to what Caleb said about our land," she began. "Couldn't there be something of value here?"

Jeffrey pushed his chair back from his desk, stretching out his legs. "I sincerely doubt it."

"But Dad, Caleb wouldn't have advised us to dig deeper if there wasn't anything."

She had a point, thought Jeffrey. An angel had made the suggestion, and he had ignored it. Realizing the serious error he had made, he said: "You're right. I'll make some calls to find out how much it would cost to bring in an expert to complete a rock and soil sample analysis."

Then it happened. Casey's cell phone rang, the one Caleb had given her. She stood at her father's desk, staring wide-eyed at him. Tapping on the accept call icon, she answered. "Kallan Temporary Staffing Solutions. How can I help you?"

"Hello. My name is Deborah, Managing Director for a wellness retreat centre that specializes in weight loss. We require the services of a psychologist. Would you have someone immediately available to fill the position?"

"A psychologist?" she repeated, locking eyes with her father. He gave her two thumbs-up. "Yes, that would be me, and I'm available," she replied as she reached for a pen and paper. She was amazed her voice didn't belie the nervousness she felt as she wrote down the details. When the conversation ended, she flopped down on the office chair, holding the pad of paper with slightly trembling hands. "I'm expected tomorrow, officially to start the following day," she announced with trepidation, "as a psychologist, at a weight loss retreat centre!"

GROUP DISCUSSION QUESTIONS

1. Why is giving praise and thanks so powerful?

2. There are many verses in the Bible referencing grace. Choose a Bible verse on grace to share with your group.

3. a) Jeffrey called on the Holy Spirit to intercede for him. What does the word *intercede* mean?

    b) Read Romans 8:26-27. How does the Holy Spirit intercede for us?

4. a) It's human nature to have negative thoughts. The challenge is not having them snowball into larger, darker and self-defeating thoughts. Share a time when negativity seemed to be all-consuming for you.

b) How were you able to move out of it? If negativity continues to consume you, what steps can you make to help you move forward?

5. a) Caleb told Casey that "being average doesn't define a person. What does is how they use their natural talents and spiritual gifts." What is the difference between natural talents and spiritual gifts?

b) Share what you see are your talents and gifts.

6. Caleb stated, "There are no superheroes in the Bible. Only ordinary people who did extraordinary things because of their belief."

a) Name a Bible character who did something extraordinary. What did they do?

b) How might Caleb's statement apply to you?

c) Explain a time when you had to do something you felt was outside your ability or your skill level? How did you feel? How did you get through it?

7. Do you have observations or questions that arose from reading *Things To Be Grateful For?* Discuss them with your group.

Prayer Time Direction

❖ Give thanks that you are dearly loved by your heavenly Father, just as you are.
❖ Thank the Holy Spirit for interceding during times when you felt distressed, worried, hopeless, or overwhelmed.
❖ Pray for any concerns that group members identified.
❖ Pray for an attitude of gratefulness.
❖ Give praise that you are not alone. Not only do you have the Father, Son, and Holy Spirit on your life team, but also your Christian family and friends.

GEMSTONES

THINGS THAT
ARE MISSED

CHAPTER 1

Casey Kallan drove her trusty old car down the gravel road, dust clouds briefly following in its wake. In the last hour, she'd had to adjust the sun visor to shade her eyes from the late afternoon glare and set the air conditioner temperature to a more comfortable level. According to the GPS, her destination was near. This stretch of roadway was much quieter than the busy highway she'd left earlier. No longer did she have to focus on race-type drivers weaving in and out of traffic. What did require her full attention was wildlife; not an uncommon occurrence when one drove through the foothills of the Rocky Mountains. As her eyes took in the picturesque scenery, her ears listened to the final chapter of an audio mystery novel played from her cell phone, rerouted through the car's speaker system. It certainly helped pass the time as she drove up and down hills, zigzagging her way through the landscape. The novel ended just as she crested a hill, The Wellness Retreat Centre in sight. The panoramic view - breathtaking.

The log-built structure sat in the middle of green space, surrounded by woods on three sides. A farmer's field, ladened with canola plants, bumped up against the west side, their yellow flowers a stark contrast against the various hues of green from the forest it bordered and the azure-coloured sky that seemed to rest upon it. "Spectacular artwork, God," Casey acknowledged as she began the descent down the steep hill.

Minutes later, she had parked her car alongside The Centre's shuttle van. She retrieved her floral suitcase from the trunk and pressed the key fob icon to lock all doors. Casey had no sooner secured the car when she wondered why she even bothered, as The Centre was located in the middle of nowhere. Having extended the suitcase handle, she proceeded to tow it across the gravel driveway, her hand vibrating in response to the wheels that bumped and rattled over it. A brisk tug got it over the wooden lip of the porch ramp; the wheels immediately silenced.

Standing before the entrance door, Casey readjusted her blazer jacket and lightly brushed the bits of dust off her pants. She took a deep, calming breath before pushing the doorbell. She was ready. Ready to begin her first official assignment.

Patiently she waited for someone to open the beautiful oak door, but no one came. She pressed the doorbell again. Still no answer. "Maybe they'll hear this," she said as she lifted the ornate beaver door knocker. Thwack, thwack, thwack echoed the sound amid the background of nature's whispers. Several minutes passed before more strikes of the beaver's tail to the bronze plate were made. She surveyed the area to the right and left of her, hoping to spot movement. But there was not a soul in sight. "Where is everyone?" she wondered aloud. Trying the doorknob, she found it unlocked. Hesitating mere seconds, she entered, justifying the intrusion by her being an employee of The Centre. Immediately, Casey felt as if she had walked through an invisible barrier. "Ah, that's how you planned it, God," she murmured with relief. "I wondered how I was to know when you'd provide me with the skills and knowledge needed for this assignment. Thank you."

As Casey stood in the foyer, she gazed about the posh surroundings. This place was a luxurious wellness centre, which would explain why no prices had been posted on the internet. From the adjoining room, a cascade of voices floated in. Due to the time of day, she assumed the people were having their evening meal, the likely reason no one heard the multiple raps upon the main door.

Leaving the suitcase in the entranceway, Casey stepped into the living room, taking a three-sixty turn. The room was beautifully designed by an architect and tastefully decorated by an interior designer. A large, natural stone fireplace dominated the main wall in the room. The art that hung above its mantelpiece was of the Dolomites mountain range in Italy, painted in acrylic. Every furniture piece was distinctive and of high quality. Tied back from the picture window were the ceiling-to-floor pinch-pleated drapes. There were potted flowers, primarily orchids, throughout the room, their colours harmonizing the room's lavish décor.

Hearing approaching footsteps, Casey turned just as a well-dressed woman entered. The woman stopped in her tracks, her eyes darting about as if checking who else may be lurking about. "And you are?" she asked sharply.

"Casey. No one responded to the doorbell or the beaver tail's raps," she said with a teasing grin, "and as the door was unlocked, I let myself in."

The woman visibly relaxed. "The doorbell's not working, and neither is the motion sensor chime that alerts us when the entrance door has been opened. I've got a couple of maintenance men working on it as we speak. They mentioned something about faulty wiring or a blown breaker. I'm Deborah, Managing Director," she announced as she walked towards her. "Welcome."

"Thank you," Casey said, shaking Deborah's outstretched hand.

"Did you have any difficulty finding the place?"

"No, your instructions were clear and concise."

"You're quite young to be a psychologist," Deborah noted. Casey acknowledged the statement but said nothing more. "Have you had dinner? We've just finished; however, I'm sure our chef can contrive to come up with something hot and savoury for you."

"Kind of you to offer, but not necessary as I had my meal before I headed out."

"I'll show you to your room then." As they made their way past the front door, Casey retrieved her suitcase. "Our centre is a two-story, built in a U-shape design," Deborah explained as she walked down a corridor to the right of the main entrance. "You entered our living room area. To the left of it are our dining room and kitchen, the only sections with no upper level. Further down are the classrooms, exercise room, and spa room, all housed on the lower level. Most of the staff offices are on the second floor."

They had reached the stairwell door at the corridor's end. "Upstairs are the staffs' bedrooms," Deborah expounded as she punched in the code to unlock the door. "You'll find the code for this door written on a slip of paper in your room. Memorize it; don't take it with you," she insisted. "It ensures your safety and privacy, and that of the other staff.

"The majority of the staff are all housed at the centre," continued Deborah as they climbed the wooden steps. "I'm one of a few that drive home each evening. The clients' quarters are on the main floor, directly below us." They had reached the second floor, where the sun's rays filled the hallway courtesy of the floor-to-ceiling window at the far end. "Laundry machines are located midway down the hallway. Across from it, you'll find a comfortable sitting area, complete with a library, printer, and computer stations. Feel free to check those areas out later."

Deborah opened the door to room number twenty-two, revealing a generous size bedsitting room furnished with a recliner chair, tallboy bureau, nightstand, and a double bed. Fixed to the wall above the bureau was a small flat-screen television. The door at the far end opened into an ensuite.

"Our therapist gave birth six weeks prematurely," Deborah volunteered while watching Casey remove her car keys from her jacket, placing them on the nightstand. "We had arranged for her maternity leave replacement to have a couple of weeks overlap. Unfortunately, the other therapist was unable to come any earlier than was previously arranged. We're grateful that you were available on such short notice."

"The best laid plans of mice and men often go awry," Casey quoted absently from John Steinbeck's book, Of Mice and Men, while lifting her suitcase onto the bed. She glanced over at Deborah, noting her blank face. "Well-planned contingency scenarios can go wrong, especially when babies are involved as they wait for no one." Casey was about to unzip her suitcase but thought better of it. She turned to give the Managing Director her undivided attention but was waved off to continue unpacking.

Deborah smiled indifferently to her remark. "What is fortunate is that you'll be starting with a new group of ladies rather than having to come in mid-session. Do take the opportunity to enjoy some of the amenities we offer here." She proceeded to describe, in detail, the attributes of The Centre. The manner in which Deborah spoke made Casey feel as if she were a client rather than a staff member.

"The room is charming," Casey stated while she moved items into a dresser drawer.

"I'm so glad you think so," Deborah acknowledged with pride, "as I had to convince Dr. Alisha to allow me to purchase specific items that I felt would convey a cozier atmosphere."

"Who is Dr. Alisha?" she inquired as she hung up clothing items into the closet, organized by colour.

"Founder of The Wellness Retreat Centre, CEO, and the resident doctor. Her full name is Dr. Alisha Mukhopadhyay. You can understand why we call her Dr. Alisha. She divides her time between The Centre and her in-town private practice."

"Are there other doctors here as well?" Casey asked inquisitively.

"No. A locum comes in when Dr. Alisha is away attending a conference, on holidays, or is ill, which she rarely is. We have a full-time nurse on duty," Deborah supplied, abruptly ending further questions when she noticed the time on her exquisite watch. "Come along. I'll give you a tour of the facility. After that, the evening is yours as I've some other business to attend to before I can go home." Casey closed the lid on her near-empty suitcase and obediently followed her employer out of the room.

The tour was a brief one. Deborah took her through the hallway that led to the various offices and activity rooms. She introduced her to the few staff they crossed paths with, and although Deborah acknowledged the clients they ran into with a simple greeting, she didn't bother to introduce any of them to Casey.

As they passed rooms, Deborah rambled off the name of whose office it was or the room's purpose as if Casey were incapable of reading the signage on the doors. They stopped before the door labelled Group Room 1. Deborah pressed the numbers to the keyless lock, then held the door open for her. "Your classroom. The door at the rear leads to your private office." She moved aside so her new psychologist could step in to have a better look.

Another pricey and tastefully decorated room, thought Casey. The exterior wall was an expansive glass wall, exposing a manicured lawn bordered by the foothills forest. A large whiteboard hung on one wall, and various artworks filled the other two. Mounted on the ceiling was a projector. The chair models were not the typical classroom stacking chairs. These were all-steel frame leather chairs with thick, four-inch padding. There were two sizes: single and extra-large. Casey turned the doorknob to her office. Locked.

"Maintenance will reprogram the code tonight," Deborah promised from the doorway. "It'll be the same number as your bedroom code, and like all the doors in this centre, they automatically lock when closed. Now, come along. Time is ticking."

Casey fast-walked out of the room, closing the door behind her. She hoped she could keep her clients focused on her teachings rather than gazing out the windows to the scenic outdoors. She followed mutely behind the Director. In short order, they had returned to where they had begun - the living room.

"Breakfast is at 7:30. Staff sit at the dining room tables along the back wall. Do you remember how to get back to your room?" Casey nodded. "Good. See you in the morning."

What a ritzy place this is, thought Casey as she climbed the stairs to the second level. She entered the assigned code to her room and, once inside, rested her back against the closed door. A wave of panic swept over her. Trudging to her bed, she plopped onto its edge, planting her head into her open hands. "Oh, God. What am I doing here? I'm not a therapist! These upscale women aren't going to accept young, unworldly me! She flopped back on her bed, staring blankly up at the ceiling with dewy eyes. "The shoes you are asking me to fill are too big! I feel incompetent, unworthy, and alone like Moses did when you called on him to lead your people." Casey jerked up straight, wiping a tear away with the back of her hand. "Wait. Not unworthy, for you chose me. Me! Not alone, for I have you, Jesus. Please, Lord, release the fear and doubt that grips me. Replace it with trust, confidence, and hope." She spent the next hour in prayer and reading passages from Exodus and commentaries on Moses.

Casey was up early the following day to get a walk in before breakfast. In the kitchen, she introduced herself to Chef Emma, who was busy making the morning meal with her kitchen staff. She asked the chef about her work while she visited the tea trolly, choosing a fruity-flavoured herbal teabag to drop into her travel thermos followed by hot water from the thermal carafe. They chatted a few minutes longer before she forced herself to leave the heavenly aromas of freshly baked bread.

"Help yourself to an apple from the basket on the counter," Chef Emma called out as Casey strolled towards the door.

There were several varieties. Casey chose a Granny Smith apple and took a delicious bite from it. "Thanks," she called out, waving the apple in the air as she headed for the exit.

Not long after having entered the woods, Casey pitched the apple's core into the depths of it. She had been following a path, which eventually led her to a lookout point overseeing the Rockies, the morning sky being the canvas backdrop. Here, in the quietness, she prayed for courage and direction. She made a promise to herself to return here each morning, having found it to be the perfect place to pray and reflect.

As she turned to head back, she noticed a heap of rocks covered with a layer of leaves and twigs. Mixed in were dandelions and thistles, their roots buried in the soil-filled crevices. The stones appeared to be remnants of the half-wall built to protect observers from falling into the gully below. She thought it to be a pity that the mound had not been removed as it distracted from the area's natural beauty.

Back in her room, Casey quickly changed into professional attire before taking the stairs to the main level. Entering the dining room area, she found it buzzing with conversations from the forty overweight women and staff members that filled it. She joined the queue at the buffet table, not having to stand in line long before being able to pick up an earthenware plate and small bowl from the stacked piles. While scooping yogurt into her bowl, she overheard Deborah reprimanding a client.

"Jessica, dear. Your plate is a little full, don't you think? And where's the fruit?"

"Oh, it's there," maintained the lady. "Buried under the pancakes."

Deborah used a fork to lift the pancakes soaked in syrup. "Two blueberries don't meet the stated meal requirements," she frowned, "and neither do the slabs of butter you've buried alongside them. Don't think I didn't notice the extra pancake hidden between the other two. Try again," she insisted as she took the plate, dumping the contents into the garbage can.

"But I'm ravishing!" came the huffy tantrum. "What you expect us to eat wouldn't sustain a rabbit."

"Changing your eating habits won't be easy," Deborah acknowledged. "It's one of the reasons, however, why you are here – accountability." She handed her a clean plate, directing her to start again.

A middle-aged lady stood beside Casey at the buffet table. "A starvation diet, that's what she's really recommending," claimed the woman with a British accent. "I know how she feels."

Casey was waiting for her toast to pop from the machine.

"Take a banana corn muffin," she quietly suggested to Mandy, having read her name tag. "It'll make you feel fuller."

"I highly doubt it," came the angry retort. "Besides, what would skinny young you know about hunger? Your stomach is probably the size of a pea! I may need to lose several stones, but I don't intend to do it by starving myself," she retorted before leaving for her table.

Casey heard a loud ping sound when the word 'stone' was spoken. She looked around to see if anyone else had heard it. Obviously not as conversations continued uninterrupted. She briefly raised her eyes heavenward. Message received, she said silently. She's my gemstone client, my assignment.

CHAPTER 2

Casey felt uneasy at having learned that Mandy was God's chosen one, the one she was to help shine from the inside-out. Again, she questioned God's chosen servant choice, but He had chosen her, and she had obediently answered the call. The doubts that had seeped into her mind were quickly dispelled, having recalled the angel Caleb's reassuring words: 'God will give you the skillset required for the assignment' and 'you are never alone.' I'm not alone, she repeated to herself.

With her confidence restored, Casey stood before the buffet table, reading the card signs that named the types of omelettes inside the food pans of the chafer dish. How was it possible for women to lose weight at this centre with the array of delectable dishes presented, she wondered. Reaching for a silicone spatula, Casey lifted a mushroom omelet placing it on top of the toast on her plate.

"Don't take what Mandy said to heart," whispered a young lady who had pulled down the roll-top chafer cover for Casey. "She's venting her frustrations. It's not unusual for some clients to feel they're making sacrifices rather than lifestyle changes.

They all get it, eventually. I'm Teresa, by the way, the Exercise Specialist, and you must be our replacement psychologist." She escorted Casey to the employees' table, and once seated, Teresa introduced Casey to the staff. Those around the table then proceeded to introduce themselves.

"Are any of these women repeat offenders?" Casey asked while raising a spoon of yogurt to her mouth.

"Would you believe almost a third of them are?" came the reply from the nurse. Casey's eyes widened. "For them, this place serves a dual purpose: weight loss and sanctuary. They're here to lose pounds but also to be pampered and to escape spouses, children, and required duties of their rich and famous lives. They arrive alone or with their group of girlfriends."

Casey stole a glance at Mandy, sitting among a table of ladies who spoke loudly and with animation. She had inclined an ear to the lady speaking next to her. "And the woman with the British accent, the one I met at the buffet table. Has she been here before?"

"No, she's new," replied the dietitian. "And, from what I read about her, she's not from the old money family."

Casey scraped the remnants of the yogurt in her bowl. "What's inherited money got to do with anything?"

"Watch for cliques forming as they divide themselves into exclusive groups," replied the dietitian. "You'll notice a pattern. I sincerely doubt she'll be in the 'old money' group."

Deborah reminded the team about not fraternizing with the clients and the signed confidentially agreement pertaining to photos, messaging, and the like. Casey felt this was primarily directed at her, as Deborah kept looking her way. "Retain your professional roles, 24/7. Is that understood?" Each staff member nodded their assent, Casey included.

"Expect Deborah to keep reminding you of your place

around here," Teresa said as they strolled down the hallway towards the business wing. "If she finds you've broken any of her golden rules, you'll be out the door in no time flat. Be careful," Teresa warned before changing the subject.

"On the first day of classes, all the women are to meet in your classroom," began Teresa. "There, they'll divide themselves into three groups, and they'll remain in those groups for the duration of their stay. A third stays with you, a third leaves with me, and the rest accompany the dietitian. After our one-hour session ends, their schedule has them moving on to their next class. They spend the last hour of the morning attending individual sessions with a professional or pursuing leisure activities such as massages, soaking in the hot tub, reading, or whatever else. A similar scenario replays in the afternoon."

"And the doctor's visits?"

"Dr. Alisha meets with them on an as-needed basis. She has this centre running like a well-oiled machine, which means we're not to deviate from her schedule." They had entered the classroom where the women were milling about, a few standing in self-appointed groups.

"We can't allow these cliques to form," insisted Casey, speaking in a low voice to her colleague.

"Don't upset the applecart," cautioned Teresa, noting the dietitian was conspicuously absent. As they took their place at the front of the room, she added, "They won't like you usurping them."

"You think?" winked Casey. Teresa visibly tensed.

"Ladies, may we have your attention?" called out Casey. She waited for their chattering to end; a few were oblivious to her request and annoyed at the members who shushed them. "My name is Casey, and I'm your therapist. You'll be joining me for daily group sessions, as well as individual sessions during the week. You will be divided into three groups ..." She was interrupted as the women began migrating into their chosen subgroup. "… by myself and Teresa," she emphatically finished.

"I don't think so," retorted a woman in her fifties wearing a bright pink outfit. "We'll be the ones choosing," she said, flashing a sweet smile to the women surrounding her.

"No, you won't," Casey replied with calm authority. Some of the more vocal ladies vehemently voiced their feelings on the matter.

Teresa moved to stand face-to-face before Casey. "What are you doing?" she hissed. "Trying to get us fired?"

"Do you think we'll be successful if they're the ones running the show?" queried Casey as she gave a quick scan of the women that sat with their preferred group. The pink-dressed lady appeared to be leading the conversation with her kindred group, her crescendo voice dominating all others in the room. "Trust me. I know what I'm doing." Resigned, Teresa agreed to follow her lead. "But first, I need you to go through this list and identify the ones you know to be in alliance with one another." Teresa hastily drew lines connecting clique members. "Great. Now, stand beside me to show support, but for goodness' sake, don't disagree with me, or we'll both lose face."

Casey again requested the room's attention. She had every intention of splitting apart the rebels. "We've decided on each group's membership. When I call your name, proceed to your assigned group. Stand by the door if you're in the dietitian's class, along the sidewall if you're in the exercise specialist's group or take a seat if you're with me."

"We're already in our groups, so let's get on with it!" declared the lady whose complexion had become as pink as her outfit.

Ignoring the outburst, Casey walked confidently around the room. "Titles, occupations, and social status have meaning out there, in the materialistic world," she said, pointing a finger to the outdoors. "Here, in the world of health and wellness, they have no value whatsoever. You came here because you wanted professional help to reverse the slide your body has taken. Isn't this true?" She saw a few heads nod. "You've lost control. Teresa and I, and the rest of The Centre's staff, are here to help you get it back. To do this, you need to let go of your defences. You also need to concede that staff are the experts in the wellness area, which means they deserve your respect."

Casey was amazed at her confidence level and that she had attained control of the room; the room was silent with all eyes on her. "We're going to challenge you to stretch your physical and mental self. You've heard the phrase, 'out with the old, in with the new.' Well, that's one of the goals we hope you will reach by the end of your stay. We're going to help you dispel the old, unhealthy ways you've been thinking and behaving and replace them with healthy thoughts, activities, and habits. It's not going to be an easy road to travel. It'll be emotionally taxing and physically gruelling, but you won't be alone on your journey. You have a team of professionals, and like-minded individuals, walking alongside you." Looking at Teresa, she gave her a huge grin, "We journey together, right?"

"Right!" responded Teresa.

Casey then turned to the group, repeating the question, her arm raised high, her fist clenched: "We journey together, right?"

The ladies raised their fists, responding in unison: "Right!"

"That's what I want to hear, a commitment to yourself and those around you. Everyone, please stand up."

As the group stood, the dietitian ran into the room, apologizing for her tardiness. "I spilt coffee over myself and needed to make a quick change." She took her place beside Casey and Teresa.

Casey read from her list, consigning each person to a group. Five minutes later, Teresa and the dietitian escorted their chatty group of ladies out of the room. Casey requested her group of women to bring their chairs in to create a circle. Pink Lady, Casey's private nickname for Patricia, seemed to have settled to the fact that she had lost this battle. She begrudgingly dragged her chair into the circular formation.

"I'm sure you've all heard of icebreaker games," Casey began amongst groans from the group. "Don't fret. I'm not going to have you engage in Minute-To-Win-It game show challenges or anything similar to it. What I want you to do is stand, introduce yourself, and then name two take-out items." Casey grinned at the group. "I'm not referring to restaurant food. I want you to identify two objects you would take out of your home if it were engulfed in flames. It can't be photos, and it can't be alive, like a person or a pet. I'll begin. My name is Casey Kallan. I'd rescue my high school track running medal and a charm bracelet."

As the women each took a turn, they appeared captivated at the choices expressed. Casey knew they would because disclosure always revealed a deeper layer than the superficial one people showed. She stood again when the last person shared her take-out items. "Thank you for participating in this exercise. Did anyone catch the similarities? No? The two objects you all described were sentimental items as opposed to pragmatic ones: a child's handprint in clay, grandmother's wedding ring, your stamp collection, the homemade quilt. What you chose not to gather were things like your passport, laptop, cell phone, or medications." She paused, wanting to get the next point across. "You chose with your heart, not your mind. And it sounds to me that your heart made some excellent selections." She returned to her seat. "Let's spend the remainder of today's session talking about negative body image."

The ladies openly shared what it meant to them, both physically and emotionally. They shared the ups and downs with their moods. "And if one more so-called friend blames this on menopause, I'm going to shake them till their teeth start rattling!" declared Patricia. They howled at the image it elicited.

More laughter ensued as they discussed the clothes purchased in an attempt to hide their excess weight: undergarments like corsets, bodysuits, and firm control slips, high-waisted pants, flowing tops to hide the belly rolls, and full or three-quarter length sleeves to hide the flabby arms. They chortled at the list of tummy-control clothes they possessed: underwear, dresses, pants, and swimsuits. Casey laughed too, but she was also sad for them. Sad for the money outlaid to purchase items in the hopes of deceiving onlookers, and sad for the choices made to mitigate the damage to their self-esteem.

As the group filed out the door, Casey reviewed the morning's session. She gave herself a mental pat-on-the-back and a heavenward thanks, as her first session as a health psychologist had gone relatively well. She had allowed them to discuss their clothing collection longer than she had initially intended, as it seemed to aid in the group's cohesiveness. It would take time for the women to build the trust required to share vulnerabilities comfortably. Yet, time was in short supply as the women were here for two weeks, a challenge for any group work facilitator. Today had been a good session as everyone seemed genuinely engaged, everyone that is but Mandy, who remained reserved and aloof.

The women arrived punctually for their daily group sessions with Casey. If she had to rate them on social connectedness, they'd receive high scores. The level of engagement and openness would be in the low-to-mid-range. They were a reserved bunch that chose to play it safe by selecting the same individuals whenever they had to participate in group activities. She decided to try a different tactic, engaging them in a role-playing exercise whereby she assigned the pairing. Patricia and Mandy were genuinely surprised and annoyed at being partnered.

Casey started the group with a ten-minute exercise whereby one was the manager of a coffee shop and the other a disgruntled patron because a barista had spilt a few drops of the hot drink on their hand. Each individual in the team received one instruction, which they weren't to divulge to the other. Managers could not offer anything more than a free cup of coffee as compensation. Patrons were to argue for a gift certificate.

She watched as the minute hand counted down the last few seconds before she called a stop to the exercise. Besides being hilarious to watch, it attained the results she was looking for: full participation and fluid interactions. "If you had been an observer of this process, you would have been astounded at the acting abilities you all possess. Well done, and congratulations! You've just participated in your first assertiveness exercise and passed with flying colours." They spent the remainder of their time discussing how it felt in the role they played.

When Casey wasn't facilitating during the daily sessions, she was teaching, coaching, or counselling. As a facilitator, she had the challenging task of keeping the conversations balanced, drawing out those who preferred to listen while limiting the chronic talkers. As a teacher, she spoke about the damage stress could do to their minds, souls, and bodies. She talked about the importance of real, as opposed to superficial friends, and the value of having something to do, such as a hobby or volunteering, to give oneself a sense of purpose and accomplishment. As a coach, she encouraged and motivated them to practice their learnings. As a counsellor, she spent private time with each of them, listening to the reasons that fed their negative behaviours and attitudes and identifying barriers that blocked their progress. "It's the journey that's important," Casey continuously reiterated.

What that journey entailed for her gemstone client, Casey hadn't the foggiest idea. Nothing out of the ordinary emerged from their counselling sessions. Mandy's father raised her after a tragic accident had killed her mother. The death hadn't affected her as she'd been only a few months old. Her father's death, however, did upset her and rightly so. He had died a few years ago, and they had been very close. She missed his embraces, his phone calls, and his advice. He had been her anchor throughout her life, including when she left home to attend university and when she relocated to another city to start her first job. He was both a father and a friend. Casey concluded that Mandy's grieving experience appeared normal; there was nothing to indicate she remained stuck in her recovery. Mandy claimed his death was the only emotional trauma she suffered in her life. Casey had yet to find a behaviour or mental health issue that could be linked to her obesity. Exasperated, she prayed: Heavenly Father, show me what I'm missing!

Midweek the women went on a hike through the forest that surrounded the centre. A couple of staff members led the group while Casey and Teresa took up the tail-end, encouraging the stragglers onward. "I'm finding the women are participating in activities, but I don't find their hearts fully committed," Casey whispered.

"Isn't that to be expected?" countered Teresa in a soft voice.

Casey slackened the pace to create a larger gap between them and the dawdlers. "Yes and no. They arrive here with high hopes that they'll lose their goal weight and then sink into despair when they recognize it's not going to happen. We teach them that it's not a numbers game but a lifestyle change to develop a healthy body, mind, and spirit. They're completing their exercise routines, eating healthy, and understanding the concepts of lifestyle change, but it's not enough because what they're doing is action without heart."

"Without a committed spirit, you mean." Casey flashed a sideways glance at Teresa. Was she referring to the psyche or faith? "And how do you propose to address this aspect of their well-being?" her colleague asked. "Do you plan to bring in a priest or rabbi?"

Casey chuckled. "No, nothing that drastic."

"What then?"

"A labyrinth. There's a lot of benefits associated with walking one."

"A labyrinth?" asked Teresa. "You think they need to go through a maze to find spiritual wellness?"

"It's not a maze! A maze has dead ends, a puzzle that needs to be solved. A labyrinth is a one-way, meandering path that leads to its centre. The only puzzle that needs to be solved is the one within them. It's supposed to help re-centre one's heart and soul."

"Sounds like something you do in a yoga class, which this place already offers," Teresa stated as she brushed a branch out of the way. "Besides, where would we take them to experience this labyrinth? We're in the middle of nowhere."

"Well," Casey said mischievously. "We could make one."

Teresa stopped dead in her tracks, stunned at hearing such a preposterous idea from someone she had thought to be level-headed. "Make one? You're kidding, right?"

Casey burst out laughing as she shook her head. "If you could see the look on your face!" she said as she tried to duplicate Teresa's mouth-opened, deadpan face. She held her facial pose for a few seconds before collapsing into laughter.

A wide grin emerged as Teresa gently shoved her away. "We? How did I get recruited into your scheme? You dreamed it; you build it," she said as she began walking the path again.

"Oh, come on. You've seen how committed these women are to change."

"They aren't committed at all. You said so yourself."

"My point exactly! We need to try a different strategy," Casey insisted.

"There's that 'we' again."

"I can't do it without you, Teresa, or your group of women. I'd be willing to create the design, but we need manpower or rather women-power, to build it. I thought we might use those stones piled by the embankment."

"I must admit, they're an eyesore, a blight to the natural beauty around them."

Casey stepped over a tree root. "They appear to have been there for eons."

"Not that long," Teresa laughed, "four, maybe five years. The Centre had been closed during a renovation blitz. Dr. Alisha had hired a landscape company for the gabion wall installation. It was a huge project as the crew had to install support columns deep into the earth, maneuver large, wired cages into position, then fill them with stones. What Lookout Point visitors see is the beautiful natural stone fence that protects them from falling over. They don't see the two tiers of gabion walls beneath them that have effectively stopped soil erosion from happening. They're standing on a reinforced wall that will last for decades. Unfortunately, the crew hadn't bothered to haul away the unused stones." Teresa became quiet as she contemplated the idea. The more she thought about it, the more she liked it. "The ladies might enjoy being outdoors and lifting something other than dumbbells. But there are two hurdles to overcome: obtaining approval from Dr. Alisha and getting the buy-in from the women."

Casey was elated that Teresa was onboard with the idea. "I'll come up with a compelling argument to convince Dr. Alisha on the merits of this absolutely fantastic idea. The women, well, I'll try tack and diplomacy to convince them. What I need you to do is visit the maintenance yard. Ask one of the workers if there's a trailer we can use to pile the rocks into."

"You seem quite sure of yourself. I doubt you'll have any difficulties swaying Dr. Alisha to approve the project or the women to build it." But Teresa was wrong, on both counts.

CHAPTER 3

Casey stood in Dr. Alisha's office after the dinner meal concluded, outlining her labyrinth proposal. "How will it help the women with their weight loss?" the doctor asked while she roamed around the room, watering her plants. "It's not that they're running in and out of it." The doctor turned towards her. "I'm joking. I know what the purpose of a labyrinth is." She continued with the watering, talking all the while. "We offer yoga classes, although not everyone attends. Couldn't you persuade them to join it or offer guided visualization therapy or some other form of reflective therapy?"

"It's not the same," Casey asserted. "This type of psychotherapy requires that they walk the labyrinth while contemplating the challenges I give them. It's an introspection exercise to stretch and develop their minds to attain increased self-awareness and self-understanding. Afterward, they are to reflect on their experience through journaling and group discussion."

The doctor placed the watering can on a shelf, retrieving the small wastebasket and scissors beside it. "I'm sorry, Casey, but our clients have an array of classes from which to choose. I don't see the benefit of adding one more to the list," she said as she snipped off dead leaves and stems, depositing them into the wastebasket.

"It wouldn't be an optional activity; I'd incorporate it into my class time."

"It sounds too new-agey."

Casey drew in a calming breath. "Labyrinths have ancient roots, dating back more than thirty-five hundred years. They've been found in almost every continent on items like rock carvings, Greek pottery, and floors of medieval cathedrals. Studies confirm the use of labyrinths in various cultures and religions over the eons." She couldn't believe she said all of that. *You gave me archeology knowledge, God? She shook her head. Of course, you did.*

"Okay, they're not new-age," conceded Dr. Alisha as she set about manicuring her bonsai tree.

"No, they're not," Casey confirmed. "Today, there are thousands of labyrinths around the world, located in private and public places. Many churches have them inside their buildings, hospitals too. Our own Children's Hospital has an indoor one. The Seidman Cancer Centre in Ohio, and Maggie's Centre attached to Ninewells Hospital, Scotland, have outdoor labyrinths. Then there are the various retreat and renewal centres."

"I get your point. You can stop with the history lesson," Dr. Alisha said. Having finished her plant managing tasks, she returned to sit in her leather chair behind the contemporary desk gesturing to Casey to take a seat in the chair across from her.

But Casey chose to remain standing as she continued her arguments. "There's the scientific benefit to consider. Studies have linked the labyrinth to better health care outcomes." She pulled out pieces of paper from the file folder she'd be holding and placed them on the desk. The doctor picked them up, and without taking her eyes off the page she was reading, directed her to take a seat. This time, Casey complied.

"I see you've highlighted sections within the studies," Dr. Alisha noted as she perused the documents in her hand. Silence ensued as she read one particular article. It reported that the mental health clients attributed their recovery to the labyrinth and associated activities. The doctor rose, stepping away from her desk to look out her window to the backyard, an expanse of green space. After several minutes had elapsed, she asked: "How many feet does your labyrinth require?"

Casey did a happy dance from her chair. Replying to the doctor's back, she placidly said, "Thirteen meters will make an eleven-circuit labyrinth; eleven circles enclosing ten paths or what are referred to as circuits."

"And if I change my mind?" the doctor asked, turning away from the window.

"Disassemble it. However, I think you'll find it to be an enhancement to your centre."

"Very optimistic of you. How long do you expect the construction of it to take?"

Casey ticked off the items on her fingers as she spoke. "Create the design, stake it out, and relocate the stones." She fixed her eyes back on Dr. Alisha. "Three days. Maybe less, maybe more. Everything depends on how fast the women work. I can guarantee you one thing. They'll be enjoying the spa services afterward."

"Without a doubt," Dr. Alisah said, smiling. "When do you propose to start?"

"The night is yet young," she replied, nodding to the light that flowed through the window. "I'll see who I can recruit to help out."

"I'll speak with Deborah in the morning to bring her up to speed. Good luck with the project."

Casey was heading towards the door when she did an about-turn. "I'll need a few items such as masking tape, rope, and spray cans."

The doctor rolled her eyes. "What those items have to do with a labyrinth, I don't even want to know. I'm sure one of the maintenance workers can help you find the supplies you require."

Casey ran up the log-hewn flight of stairs to her room. Flipping open her laptop, she entered the password and Googled instructions for building a labyrinth. Having selected the print icon, she dashed to the floor's office room where the sole printer hummed as it spewed out the design. Casey held tightly onto the paper as she scampered down the steps to the main level. She caught sight of Teresa heading into the living room with a novel clasped in her hand.

"Teresa!" she called out.

The exercise specialist spun around. Seeing Casey's lit-up face, she slapped her book against her leg. "You convinced her, didn't you?"

"I sure did. Come on! I need your help," she said, pulling her colleague's arm.

"Whoa! First, tell me where we're going?" Teresa demanded, suspicious of what she was being dragged into.

"Outside, to paint circles on the lawn," Casey exclaimed, a twinkle in her eyes. "Come on!" she repeated, tugging her arm again. "We need to get hold of some spray cans and supplies." This time it was Teresa whose eyes were rolling.

Twenty minutes later, Teresa was pounding a wooden spike into the middle of a manicured lawn. She withdrew a swivel anchor bolt from her blue jean pocket, screwing it down tight to the top of the post. In the meantime, Casey held a measuring tape against a lengthy piece of rope. She wrapped masking tape around measured intersections.

"Okay. I'm about ready to make the circles, but first, I need to put on the protective items," Casey said as she walked over to where the oversized overalls, plastic goggles, and latex gloves laid in a heap on the grass. Having pulled the overalls over her clothes, she slipped the goggles over her head, allowing them to hang temporarily around her neck. She then glided her fingers into the latex gloves, stretching and pulling the latex to remove the web-hand look.

"What's next?" inquired Teresa.

"Pass me the end of that rope, would you?" As Casey placed her hand over the last taped spot on the rope, she directed Teresa to tie the other end through the eye of the swivel anchor bolt.

"What exactly are we doing?" asked Teresa, who was on her knees, threading the rope through the eye of the anchor bolt.

"Role-playing by the looks of it. Dog and master, perchance?" taunted a voice from behind them. Casey and Teresa both looked up to face their audience. Pink Lady and a handful of others had arrived, all of whom giggled at the remark.

"Isn't the leash a little long?" jibed another. "You won't obtain obedience if you provide so much leeway."

Teresa finished tying her knot before she rose and made her way back to Casey.

"What are you two doing?" queried Mandy, her curiosity piqued, having spotted the paint cans and sprayer.

"It's a surprise," Casey replied as she stepped closer to the uninvited audience.

"But it won't be if you all continue to stand here," Teresa added. The two stood their ground, arms crossed against their chest, patiently waiting for their audience to leave.

The women surrounding Pink Lady flicked questioning eyes

at her. Patricia's facial expression hardened. "Let's go, ladies," she testily said. "Clearly, there's nothing worth watching here."

As the women made their way back to The Centre, Casey redirected Teresa to their task. "I'll need the cordless paint sprayer to make the circles. Pour the black paint into its plastic container, then pass it to me." Teresa returned with the sprayer, handing it over to her. "Okay, this is what's going to happen next. I'm going to walk out the distance indicated by each taped section of the rope. I'll keep it taut as I spray down a line while walking the perimeter. It won't be a perfect circle, but it'll suit our needs," she explained.

Teresa looked behind Casey, to where the other women sauntered across the grass to The Centre's back door. "And if you do a lousy job?"

"I'll cover it up. Did we bring any green paint to match the grass?" Teresa's eyes squinted at the pile of paint cans. "I'm teasing!" she laughed. "It'll be fine." Casey lifted the safety glasses over her eyes before releasing the sprayer's safety latch. She squeezed the trigger, the nozzle squirting out the black liquid onto the grass as she began marking the outline of the innermost circle. When she neared the start of it, she ceased spraying; the circle was not to be closed. Moving her hand to the next position on the rope, she began spraying ring number two. When the sprayer started sputtering, she called out to Teresa to bring the refill.

"Are we going to finish this evening?" Teresa asked while exchanging the full container for Casey's empty one. "We might only have an hour of daylight left."

"We'll make it," Casey assured her while screwing on the container. "The spray gun makes the job go so much faster than if we had used aerosol spray cans." She returned to colouring the grass, Teresa replenishing the small paint container each time it emptied. The last circle was completed at the exact moment when the spray gun began hissing air out of the nozzle.

Teresa sent up a shout of triumph. "What perfect timing! Done at last!"

"Not so quick. I still have to mark the interior lines between the circuits." Casey pulled out her printed sheet once again. "One full container should be enough to finish the task." While she sprayed, Teresa removed the centre stake. The only sounds that filled the air were the paint sprayer's nozzle as it spewed out its liquid and the hammer sounds as Teresa worked on dislodging the stake she'd pounded, a little too firmly, into the earth.

Having completed her task, Teresa gingerly stepped over the painted grass to gather all the items to be returned to the maintenance garage. "Done!" Casey announced jubilantly. Then softly said, "Thanks for the idea, Holy Spirit!"

As the two walked back to The Centre's maintenance garage, Teresa voiced her trepidation in getting the women to cooperate. "I'll explain the purpose of the labyrinth and its therapeutic role," Casey said with fortitude. "All you need to do is explain the physical benefits and the methodology. Describe how the hand-to-hand rock transferring technique is to be performed. They'll get the message that this is a mandatory exercise, not an optional one."

"Okay. I'll give it a try," Teresa said apathetically. Casey's eyebrows rose. "Alright," came the hearty laugh. "I'll be emphatic with my message as I outline the merits of the activity. Is that what you wanted to hear?"

"Much better! We won't get their cooperation if they haven't a vested interest to support the project."

At the staff meeting, held before breakfast the following morning, the conversation centred on Casey and Teresa. "I wish you two had discussed your plans with me," admonished Deborah from across the boardroom table.

In a slightly irritated tone, Casey replied, "You didn't have the authority to approve; only Dr. Alisha did." She realized she'd spoken a little harshly. In a gentler tone, she said, "We weren't trying to undermine you. I was the one that sought out the doctor to obtain her approval because it was my idea. I knew it to be a long shot. If Dr. Alisha denied the request, then that would have been the end of it; dead-in-the-water, so to speak. When she gave her approval, I left the room feeling ecstatic. I found Teresa and compelled her to start immediately on the project with me."

From the corner of her eye, Deborah saw Teresa nodding in agreement. She sighed, her acquiescence dispersing the tension felt around the table. "Why don't you tell us more about this labyrinth? Start with the rope and paint sprayer I've heard so much about," she encouraged through the chortles from staff.

Casey turned to Teresa. "Go ahead. Share what we've been up to and what we've got planned for the next few days."

When Teresa concluded her summary report, Deborah said: "I suspect you'll meet with some resistance from the ... how should I describe them ... saucy ladies? You'll be needing our support, and as Dr. Alisha has approved it, we are all to approve it." She scanned the faces of the staff. "Understood?" Affirmations were received from everyone around the table. "Good." The meeting concluded a half-hour later, Deborah taking the lead as the group left for the dining room.

It was apparent that Casey and Teresa were the primary topic around the breakfast tables. If the gossiping women staring in their direction weren't enough of an indication, the various dog barks certainly were. Deborah, having had enough of the insensitive outbursts, stood up and took command of the room. When the noise level settled down to a few whispers, she began her speech. "Yesterday evening, two of our staff members began working on an exciting new project. A labyrinth." Instantly the room erupted in conversations. "Ladies! Quiet down, please! Thank you. How many of you know what a labyrinth is?" Two-thirds of the group raised their hands. "How many know how it's used in therapy?" A few hands remained in the air. "I'm not the expert on it; Casey is. She'll be sharing with you the purpose and benefits of it. But first, it needs to be finished."

"Why don't those two finish it themselves?" piped up Mandy. Other women chimed in their words of support, Casey noticing how Mandy seemed to relish this camaraderie.

"That's a fair question," responded Deborah. "One of the values our centre holds dear is the word, teamwork. Two people are not the full team complement required for this sort of project. We need all of you to participate. Teresa will be incorporating it in as part of your exercise program." Groans could be heard from all sides of the room. "I'm not going to say it will be easy work, but I can assure you that you will be proud of your accomplishment. You will have created this centre's first labyrinth, and you will be the first of many to experience its therapeutic worth. Don't reject this opportunity; embrace the challenge."

Several arms shot up into the air. "I won't be answering questions," Deborah flatly stated. "Casey and Teresa are the ones to ask, and not here, as this is your breakfast hour. Hold your questions until class time." Deborah sat back down, the room returning to its pre-speech noise level.

"Thanks," Casey said with sincerity.

Deborah poured milk onto her cereal. "My part was easy. I don't expect yours will be."

Not long after, Casey welcomed Teresa's and the dietitian's group into her classroom. They had rearranged their schedules, with Dr. Alisha's permission, so all the women could work together on the project. Casey proceeded to expound upon an abbreviated version of the history and benefits of labyrinths that she had relayed to the doctor not fourteen hours earlier.

"It sounds like nonsense if you ask me," commented Mandy. Others murmured their agreement.

"Don't knock it till you've tried it," countered Casey. "It really can help you to quiet your thoughts, allowing your mind to hone in on things that may be blocking you from moving forward."

"Someone seems to be getting a little testy," said Patricia, chuckling lightly at fellow cronies, who responded in kind.

"And trying awfully hard to convince us of its merits," added Mandy.

"I'm not trying to convince you as much as I'm trying to have you understand its purpose," Casey stated evenly. "If you go in with a closed mind, then I can guarantee you that you'll find it a useless exercise. If you step into it with an open mind, then you allow yourself the possibility of something to change within your inner self. Teresa?"

"Thanks, Casey. This afternoon, we will start with phase one of the labyrinth project - carrying the stones from the pile at Lookout Point and depositing them into two small trailers. A maintenance employee will then have them brought to the green space behind The Centre. Phase two involves moving the stones again, this time from the trailers onto the painted circles on the lawn." Teresa's eyes sparkled as her audiences' eyes dimmed and their shoulders sagged.

"What about our hands?" asked a young lady, which automatically led everyone to examine their own.

"Worried about calloused hands and chipped fingernails?" asked Teresa. "Not to worry. We'll provide work gloves to protect them."

"What about our backs?" lamented Mandy. Casey refrained from laughing at their pitiful excuses.

"You'll be strengthening those weak muscles," Teresa assured them. "Isn't that what you want? To feel better than when you arrived? The stones won't be any heavier than the dumbbell weights you lift in the exercise room." Teresa and Casey spent the next half-hour fielding their questions.

"Our time is up, ladies," Casey announced. "This afternoon, you are to meet Teresa and me at the stone pile location. Wear your running shoes; no sandals will be permitted."

The women arrived at the designated area, on time and in proper outdoor attire. Casey hoped they realized their designer running shoes wouldn't remain in store-bought condition by the time they had finished constructing the labyrinth. She counted the number of women gathered around Teresa. Not one person had backed out. Amazing, thought Casey.

Teresa began by teaching the group the proper way to lift. "Back injuries occur because of improper lifting techniques. Don't bend over to pick up your stone the way you do when I ask you to reach down to touch your toes."

"What?" Mandy asked, feigning surprise. "There's someone here who can touch their toes? Show yourself!" she demanded, scanning the group that had erupted with laughter.

Teresa chuckled with them. "You are to do squats. Push back your hips and bend your knees." She proceeded to show them the proper lifting technique. "Maintain a healthy posture by keeping a straight back when going down to retrieve the stone and when coming up with it. Another important rule is that you are never to twist your body when holding something heavy. It's a recipe for lower back pain and muscle damage. When you pick up the stone, turn your whole body and then carry it to a trailer." She illustrated her instructions by modelling the steps. It concluded when the stone she carried was dropped into a metal trailer.

"Okay, it's your turn," Teresa said. "We'll start by having you divide into your preassigned groups." The women shuffled themselves into their regular groups. "Great. Group three, we need you to split into two, then join with one of the groups." When the two groups had been established, Teresa assigned them to a trailer. She then gave her final instructions. "Line up, and when ready, begin, one at a time. Casey will watch group one and me the other to ensure you're following my lifting and turning instructions. Work at your own pace; this isn't a race to see which group finishes first."

Casey and Teresa complimented the women on their lifting technique and the progress they were making. The ladies worked at a relatively steady pace, although some were a tad slower than the rest. As Mandy heaved the last stone into her trailer, cheers spontaneously broke out.

"Well done!" Teresa said, applauding. She waited for the ladies to settle down before continuing. "There's one more thing we need to do before I can dismiss you. Can anyone tell me what that is?"

"Cool-down," shouted out someone.

"That's right. This was a great workout, but like all workouts, we need to finish with stretching exercises. I'll guide you through a few. Trust me," Teresa said over the whines of the women, "you'll feel less sore and tired than if you don't do it." The women unenthusiastically followed Teresa through her cool-down routine.

"This was truly a productive day," Casey said. "Tomorrow will be too."

"What's that supposed to mean?" asked a tired Mandy.

"It means the labyrinth remains unfinished. Phase two," reminded Casey."

"No way," shouted a familiar voice. All eyes turned to Pink Lady. "Find someone else to do your grunt work!" Others stood beside her in a show of solidarity.

Casey stepped forward. "Is this how you resolve challenging tasks by deflecting responsibility?"

Patricia planted her hands on her hips. "We didn't sign up for this!"

Casey ignored the comment. "You may not have liked the workout we chose, but you did it. What we witnessed today was personal perseverance, teamwork, and success. We saw how you encouraged one another. We heard you cheer in unison when the last stone landed in the trailer. Pat yourself on the back for what you accomplished personally and as a member of your team. You've completed half the project!

"So, don't quit. Don't settle for a job that's half done," Casey pleaded. "If you do, you'll be reinforcing a habit that needs to stop. The habit of giving up because you feel it's too difficult, too painful, too overwhelming, too impossible, too … you fill in the blank. Do you know what the actor Audrey Hepburn said about the word impossible? She said, 'Nothing is impossible, the word itself says, 'I'm possible'!'"

"Ha!" snarled Patricia. "You're guilting us into completing your project."

"It's neither Teresa's or my project," corrected Casey. "It's *our* project," she said as she swept her arm before the group. "And you'll relish that fact when your collective hard work brings this labyrinth to completion. Let's finish *our* project! Meet us at the labyrinth site at nine a.m. You're all dismissed." Patricia gave a short snort. She took off her gloves and threw them on the ground before leading the weary group back to The Centre.

Teresa picked up the tossed gloves." I don't know how you do it," she said as they began their walk back, "countering their whines and complaints with pep talks and motivational speeches. I find it draining."

Casey lightly touched Teresa's arm, stopping her on the path. "Do you feel like that all the time?" she asked with concern.

"What? Oh, no, no," she laughed. "I'm not experiencing burnout if that's what you're thinking. I meant that I'm not one for inspirational speeches. My tactic is finding fun exercises to encourage participation."

"Fun exercises. Isn't that an oxymoron?" Casey asked, smiling.

"You should have been at my class yesterday when I taught them a country line dance. They appeared to be having lots of fun with that cardio workout!"

"You and I are coaches using different approaches to reach the same end goal."

"Oh, nicely said. Care to repeat it?" Teresa asked.

"Repeat it? I can't believe I even said it!" she laughed.

"Well, I liked it, Coach Casey. Now, about tomorrow. What's the game plan as I don't want any member of my team becoming a spectator?" The two broke into fits of laughter, and it continued all the way back to The Centre as each threw out witty sports analogies while devising a strategy to keep the ladies engaged.

Deborah had received the update regarding yesterday's success and the threat of non-compliance to complete the project from Casey during the early morning staff meeting. "The teamwork speech worked once, but I doubt it'll work again. I propose a different course of action." She proceeded to outline her plan.

At breakfast, Deborah stood at the front of the room, giving praise to the women for what had been accomplished. "As for completing the labyrinth, I'm going to let you decide, as a group, whether to finish it. We're going to be democratic about it. You'll be voting, anonymously, for option 1 or 2. What the majority decides goes. Here are your choices," she continued as staff handed out papers and pens. "Option 1: The stones will be moved from the trailers to the labyrinth site. Option 2: The stones will be moved from the trailers to a site by the maintenance garage. Option 1 has you completing the labyrinth, which means you will be credited for its completion and be the first group to use it. Option 2 means you've chosen the next group of ladies attending this centre to complete the work you've started. It makes no difference to me as it will be completed, with or without your help. Either way, the trailers will be emptied as the maintenance crew requires their use. It's your decision." The Director repeated the choices before handing wicker baskets to three staff members for ballot collecting.

Pink Lady smiled a knowing smile to the women sitting at the tables. She and her circle of friends had taken it upon themselves to speak to all the women encouraging them to boycott any further work on the labyrinth. Voting was an even better option as it afforded anonymity. She had hoped to have avoided a second day of manual labour, but she hadn't anticipated Deborah's alternative. It didn't matter as long as they weren't supporting Casey's project. Patricia was confident the women would choose option two, which would send a clear message to Casey about what they thought of menial work and who was really in charge.

The votes had been gathered and counted. Deborah accepted the piece of paper handed to her by a staff member. "Everyone voted; there were no abstainers and no spoiled ballots." Patricia looked smugly at Casey. "The count is thirty-four to six," announced Deborah, her face remaining expressionless, whereas Patricia's changed from smug to delighted. "Thirty-four to complete the labyrinth!" she said, her lips curling into a grin." The room exploded with excitement. Patricia slumped back in her chair. "Okay, ladies. You've made your decision. Casey and Teresa will be expecting all of you outdoors shortly, no exceptions. Good luck with your project."

The labyrinth was quickly completed, thanks to Teresa's idea of some fun, healthy competition. She had the ladies split into yesterday's team, and then they were to choose a team captain. While they were doing that, Casey and Teresa pulled a long yellow rope across the labyrinth's design, tying each end securely to a stake.

"Captains, please come forward," requested Casey. "And bring along someone for the extra pair of ears to hear the instructions." Patricia and Mandy stepped forward along with their chosen teammate. "Okay. Listen carefully. You'll have ten minutes to come up with a team name and a chant. Then comes the challenge. The goal is to complete your half of the labyrinth before the other team does. The rocks are to be placed end-to-end on top of the painted circles. I'll be taking away five seconds for unsportsmanlike conduct or incorrect transferring. Questions?"

"How much planning time are you allotting for the challenge?" asked Mandy.

"Fifteen minutes," replied Casey. "Any other questions? Right then. Go. Instruct and motivate your team. Teresa will blow the whistle for the start and end of the segments."

When the whistle blew to end the ten-minute team name exercise, Casey had the captains come forward. She pulled out a coin. "Patricia, you call it. The side you call will be up first." Patricia called out 'tails' as Casey flipped the coin into the air. It landed 'heads' up. "Mandy, your team starts."

Mandy stepped before her group. "I want it loud, on three. What's our name?" she yelled. She held up one, two, then three fingers.

"Her. Her. Her-ricanes!" came the chant.

"And why are we called Her-ricanes?"

"We blow, blow, blow the competition away." They all huffed out air towards the rival team.

"That was awesome, Her-ricanes!" said Teresa. "Patricia. Show us what your team has got!"

Patricia motioned for the ladies to line up. They stood with feet apart, fists poised as if they were in a boxing ring. "Who are we?" she asked.

"Boxing Divas!"

"And what's our chant?"

"We have speed. We'll succeed! We have mettle! We won't settle. We're the Boxing Divas!"

"Well done, Her-ricanes and Boxing Divas!" said Casey. "That was amazing considering the short time you were given. Okay. It's time for the final challenge. Captains. You have fifteen minutes to plan your strategy." Teresa pressed the start button on her stopwatch. It seemed they had just begun when they were told to stop.

"Captains," called out Casey. "Take your team to the trailer located on your side of the rope. Have them put on their work gloves and, when everyone has, raise your hand." A few minutes later, Mandy lifted hers, and seconds later, Patricia did likewise. "When the whistle blows, you will begin. Have your team stand together to indicate completion."

Teresa blew the whistle, and the women were off. Both teams had the same strategy of dividing their team in two; however, their approaches differed. The Boxing Divas worked from each end towards the middle. The Her-ricanes had group one start from the far end, working towards the centre, while the second group started at the center and worked towards the opposite end. Coaches and teammates alike shouted words of encouragement to the people in their human chain.

"Come on, ladies. Pick up the pace!" yelled Patricia. "You're as slow as molasses!"

"Placers," called out Mandy. "If your legs are feeling sore or cramped, go ahead and swap with someone." A couple of ladies exchanged positions. "That goes for you lifters, taking from the trailer, as well."

"We're good," came the reply. "Are we almost done?"

"You just keep with the steady pace," Mandy instructed. "I'll let you know when we're nearing the end." The Boxing Divas team were colliding with one another as they neared their centre. Stones were dropped, words were exchanged, and frustration mounted. Mandy quietly told her lifters to stop as the last stone made its way down the chain. Once placed, the individuals inside the labyrinth hurried back to join their group. A whistle shrieked through the air, followed by the whoops from the Her-ricanes.

The Boxing Divas had been startled into stopping by the shrill whistle. They had been absorbed with finishing their task, oblivious to how their rival team was doing. Their downcast faces conveyed the disappointment they felt.

"Patricia, is this how you're going to leave it?" asked Casey.

Patricia looked at the work that remained, then at her team. "We're not quitters! Let's finish the job!" The Boxing Divas group two women sluggishly returned to their places in the human assembly line; the stones slowly moved down it.

"Come on, Boxing Divas! You can do it," Mandy shouted. She and her team began to clap, louder and faster. The Boxing Divas group one women joined in as they rallied around their teammates. The working women's momentum and enthusiasm increased in response. Jubilant hurrahs and cheers erupted from both teams as the final stone was laid.

Dr. Alisha had crossed the lawn in time to witness the labyrinth's completion. "Remarkable!" she said, shaking the hands of those nearest her. "You should be very proud of what you've accomplished today. Gather around. I want to take a picture for posterity's sake." She had snapped a few shots before noting that Casey and Teresa remained on the sidelines. "Get over there, you two!" They declined, claiming the women deserved the recognition as they did all the work. An outcry shot out from the group resulting in a couple of ladies running over to pull them in. A few more camera clicks, and it was over.

"Don't leave yet," Casey stated as a few started to break away. "We need to announce the winner and their prize. Team captains, please step forward." She stood between Patricia and Mandy, taking hold of their wrist. All three faced the group. "The winner: Team Her-ricanes!" announced Casey as she raised Mandy's arm high. "For the next three hours, you and your team will have exclusive access to the hot tub, sauna, and masseuse! Enjoy, ladies!"

"I wonder who'll be first in line with the masseuse," mused Casey to Teresa as they moved to untie the rope and remove the stakes.

"Mandy," Teresa replied. Casey's questioning look prompted her to add, "she had the presence of mind to book a session. It was lucky for her that her team won, or else she'd have had to forfeit her spot."

When Casey commented on Mandy's foresight with the masseuse during their evening meal, she learned it was unrelated to the day's activities. She had pre-booked several spots during the week in an attempt to rid herself of headaches and chronic body pain.

It was Saturday, a day that held the same schedule as each weekday. After Casey's morning group session ended, Mandy stayed behind for her therapy session. "I've noticed you've been a little irritable these past few days. Is there something you want to talk about?" Casey asked once Mandy was seated.

"You mean people have been complaining about me," she snapped back.

"No one has," Casey assured her. "But I've found you to be more short-tempered and argumentive of late. What's going on?"

"Nothing! Can't a person have a bad day?"

"Don't you mean, days?"

Her nostrils flared. "Whatever!"

"It's not like you to lash out," Casey said in a soft tone. "What's happened?"

Mandy's aggrieved demeanour turned to contriteness. "You're right. I'm normally not such a disagreeable person," she disclosed. "The only excuses I have for being grouchy are my poor sleep and headaches, but that doesn't justify the way I've treated people of late." She stared at the carpet as she continued. "Perhaps it's time I went home."

Casey frowned. "A little drastic, wouldn't you say?"

"If I had seen some positive results, even a shred of an improvement, then I'd agree, but I haven't. I've followed every instruction explicitly, and it hasn't made an iota of a difference. No one is more disappointed than me. I couldn't accomplish one simple goal – to lose a few pounds, kick-starting my weight-loss plan. Not only have I gained weight, I feel lousier than when I arrived!"

"Give me a second while I check your records," Casey requested while opening the electronic file on her laptop. Having found the medical document she was searching for, she read the summary notes. "It says here that your family doctor cleared you of anything serious; you wouldn't be here if it were otherwise. There's no reference to migraine-like symptoms."

"He cleared me because he couldn't find anything," Mandy

began, then thought better of arguing the point. "Forget it. You're a psychologist. You probably think I'm a hypochondriac or something along those lines. It's time I packed for home," she drearily said as she got out of her chair.

"You've assumed incorrectly," Casey said, locking eyes with her. "I don't think you've made any of this up. Please stay. I want to understand."

Mandy wavered, but ultimately she wanted answers, and perhaps Casey was the one who could provide them. She sat back down. "There's not a lot to share. I've taken a battery of tests, and they've all come back negative."

"You want them to be positive?"

Mandy laughed gently. "Yes, as then I'd have something to blame, besides myself. My family doctor subtly laid the fault at my doorstep. Eat healthier; your headaches will go away. Lose weight; your breathing will improve. Use the CPAP machine; your energy level will increase. I've done everything he's recommended, but there's been no improvement!"

"Tell you what. With your consent, I'll discuss what you've shared with Dr. Alisha. Perhaps she'll have some recommendations. In the meantime, don't stop what you're doing."

The doctor, however, seemed incensed that Casey should bring up the situation with her. "I'm well aware of Mandy's issues. I get that you're concerned, but I am on top of it. I've increased her dose to help abate her headaches, and I've offered her sleeping pills, which she's refused. Staff are providing her with non-prescription intervention, such as massage, stretching exercises, and a diet that eliminates some known headache-causing triggers such as nuts and cheeses. I do hope, though, by the time this retreat draws to an end, some pounds won't be the only thing that will have disappeared."

"But what's causing them?" Casey persisted.

"I don't know. Her hypertension and diabetes seem to be well controlled. There's no organic reason, according to her preadmission medical chart. Teresa informed me that Mandy has been working hard on her exercise routine, and our dietitian stated she'd been making excellent food choices. What are your findings as to her psychological well-being? Do you find her depressed?"

Casey took some time before she responded, reviewing in her mind all that she knew of her. "No," she concluded. "I can't say she's depressed. Frustrated, yes, but not depressed. She's identified no psychological trauma that could have brought about these symptoms. She's made a few friends here, so I can't say she's isolated. These symptoms appear to have begun their downward spiral when her weight went up."

"As the cause doesn't seem to be a physical one, then likely it's psychological," asserted the doctor. "I would hazard to say that it's you who has missed something, not me. She must be holding back on a traumatic life event. Perhaps she would benefit from a psychiatric consultation," mused Dr. Alisha. "I know someone I can call in."

"Please don't. It'll certainly upset her and quite possibly destroy the thread of trust we've established. I'll continue with our therapy sessions. Perhaps there's some memory she may have subconsciously blocked that needs dislodging."

"I'll wait for your next report before I decide whether a psychiatric consult is warranted." Casey nodded, thanking the doctor for her time before leaving her office.

That night, Casey prayed for each of her clients, as was her routine. "About Mandy, Lord. Help me understand what her issues are. I sense that I'm missing something. Direct me to what it is."

CHAPTER 4

The following day, Casey had the women in her class move their chairs into a circle. "Today, we're going to delve into the source of your self-portrayal. Each of you is to share the answer to this question: Whose voice have you been listening to regarding your appearance?"

After twenty minutes of sharing, Casey summed up their responses. "You've been listening to the voices of parents, peers, producers, media, and a string of others. The one voice you all failed to mention was your own. It would seem that other people's opinions have taken precedence over your own. Why do you think that is?"

"Women have had their bodies judged by societal standards for centuries. That's not ever going to change," declared Patricia as she unzipped her sweater with the pink-flowered appliques to reveal a dusty pink silk blouse. "It's more intense for those of us in the limelight as we're targets, ripe for conversation at socials and with media critics. That's why we can't let our guard down; otherwise, we might find uncomplimentary photographs of us on the internet or grocery store tabloids."

"Being a victim is acutely felt by everyone; it isn't exclusive to your kind!" blurted out a young millennial. "You have no right to assume hurts, shame, or assaults on our appearance are any less painful than what you experience. My generation is notorious for posting images on social media platforms, which are then re-posted countless times. I've experienced humiliation when someone maliciously uploaded very unflattering photos of me onto Facebook. I know how it feels to have my weight the subject of gossipers. You're not the only one to have felt rage, rejection, and bitterness because of the treatment received at the hands of others. I have too, and it hurts big time!"

"I'm sorry," Patricia said, genuinely remorseful. "It was wrong of me to insinuate that there are two human scales to measure suffering by when there is only one." The room was stunned into silence. Pink Lady could have chosen to say nothing at all; instead, she apologized and acknowledged equalness between the social classes on this particular matter. Was the oak tree bending?

"Image is everything, and it can have emotional consequences," paraphrased Casey. She looked at each of the women sitting in her circle. "Your feelings and actions are in response to external driving sources. You're allowing them to pierce your heart and soul. Remind me. Whose voice should you be listening to?"

"Our own, of course," Mandy exasperatedly answered. "But it's not that simple."

"Actually, it is," Casey declared with absoluteness. "There's an emotional undercurrent preventing you from standing up against the voices that are not your own. And if you don't fight against it, it'll become as strong as a riptide, possibly keeping you down until your voice is forever silenced. Which emotion am I talking about?"

"Fear," volunteered the woman sitting across from her.

Casey slowly nodded. "Fear. It plays on your psyche, making you doubt yourself. It immobilizes and disempowers you. What's the fear that triggers you to listen to others' opinions?"

"Disapproval," said Patricia, "from family, friends, and even the public."

Casey sat back. "And why do you need their approval?"

"I suppose it makes us feel safe; secure in ourselves," volunteered Mandy.

"Do you honestly believe that? No, No. Don't answer that," Casey said. "It's a rhetorical question; obviously, you do. Consciously, you do care what others think. Unconsciously, you don't. You rebel by doing what you want: excess eating, overindulging in sweets, poor-to-non-existent exercise regime. In short, you self-sabotage." She uncrossed her legs, planting her hands firmly on her knees as she leaned forward. "Other people don't accept you because you don't accept yourself. Did you hear what I just said? You don't accept yourself!" she repeated.

"We accept the reality of our situations," snarled Patricia. "Society *does* judge us, and they *do* dictate whether or not we're accepted."

"What aren't they accepting?" countered Casey. "Is it your body? Your intelligence? Your skills? Your talent?"

It was Mandy who responded to the query. "When they reject our looks, they reject everything about us."

"Do they?" Casey challenged. "Instead of standing tall in the light, you've cowered into the shadows. Tell me something. Do you think less of famous singers, actors, newscasters, golfers, and other celebrities and sports stars who are overweight? Did you stop going to concerts or movies when your celeb gained weight in their career? Who am I talking about? Throw me out some names." Hesitantly the women named stars like John

Travolta, Russell Crowe, Mathew Perry, Oprah Winfrey, Kelly Clarkson, Kate Mulgrew, and others. "Did those celebrities lose their singing or acting talents because of their weight issues? No, they didn't. You want to know why? Because you accepted them as the total package. It's who they are. It's who *you* are."

Casey rose from her chair and strolled about the inner circle. "I want you to bring to mind at least one overweight person, whom you personally know and cherish despite their outward appearance." A few women smiled at the friend sitting next to them. "I know each and every one of you came up with a name. How do I know? It's quite simple. We live in an overweight society, so how can we not know someone that fits that criteria? You've made the word 'rejected' encompass everything about you. It's a word you should never allow yourselves to accept. It needs to be ejected into outer space," Casey said, kicking a make-belief item into the air. "When you walk the labyrinth today, I want you to reflect on what it will take for you to love your whole self, in the body you have right now. Tomorrow I want you to share your insights with the group." Chairs scraped the floor, and conversations flared up as the ladies made their way to the exit door.

That night, as Casey lay in bed reading, her cell phone rang. Retrieving it off her nightstand, she recognized the call display number. "Hi, Dad."

"Hi, dear. I've got an update on the rock and soil samples for our property."

Immediately she sat up. "They're done? What does the report say?"

"Whoa, girl. You've got the cart before the horse. I made some inquiries. It's going to be time-consuming, complicated, and expensive. I almost had another heart attack from the ballpark figures quoted."

Casey's shoulders slumped. "You tried, Dad."

"Hold on there. I didn't say it's a no-go. Our good neighbour, Dr. Bleviss, knows a geotechnical engineer. I just got off the phone with her and immediately rang you. Get this! She's offering her services for free! The cost we'd be responsible for is the laboratory fees and analysis report."

Casey was skeptical of any professional who offered their services for free. "What's the catch, Dad?"

"There isn't any; that's the best part! She's known Dr. Bleviss and his wife for years, and she knew about us through them. She was delighted when they approached her with the request. She wants to reciprocate the kindness they've provided her over the years by offering her services to their long-time friend and neighbour!"

"Oh, Dad. That's wonderful news! How soon?"

"She's arriving next week from Calgary and will be staying at the Bleviss's home until she's collected all the samples needed. She said it could take weeks before she receives the analysis report from the lab. That's all I have on the subject. Let's talk about you. How are things going?"

"I'm continually amazed at my facilitating skills and the medical knowledge I possess as a health psychologist. The Holy Spirit inspired me to build a labyrinth, and with the help of the exercise specialist and our clients, we completed it in two days! But as much as things are going well, I'm struggling with my gemstone client."

"How so?"

"I'm still in the dark as to what it is that I'm to help her with."

"Take the time to walk your labyrinth. Be open to the word or words the Holy Spirit makes known to you. God brought you there for a reason. He'll reveal it to you in His time."

"Sound advice. Thanks, Dad. What are my brothers up to?" Casey learned that Jason was to start a summer job as a bookkeeper at a non-profit organization, and Aaron had enrolled in 4-H Club programs. After they had said their goodbyes, Casey thought back to the days when she was in a 4-H Club. She reflected on the leadership camp she had attended, the people she met, the songs they sang around the campfire, and the water balloon battles. Amid these memories, she'd fallen asleep.

It was early morning; the mist hung in the air, the dew deposited on every exposed natural and man-made surface. Casey pulled her sweater tighter to keep warm against the cool air as she strode over to the labyrinth. Stepping into the entrance, she stood there, in the stillness of the morning, eyes closed. She breathed deeply through her nostrils, then slowly exhaled through her mouth, continuing with this calming exercise as she waited for the word or image that she was to concentrate on, to enter her mind. The word revealed: *missed*.

Crossing her arms against her to keep warm, she channelled her thoughts onto the *missed* word as she began her walk. Images flowed in and out of her mind. Missed opportunities – not attending a birthday party because she had been ill. Missed loved ones – the death of her grandfather, uncle and mother. Missed connections – friends who had moved away. Her mind drifted to the connections she did have, but she stopped them to focus on what had been missed, not on what she had. What else? Missed possessions – her favourite porcelain horse, shattered to pieces when Aaron accidentally knocked it off the shelf.

Before she knew it, Casey had walked her way into the centre of the labyrinth. She pivoted around, gazing upon the stones that outlined the centre's circle. Her eyes rested on a dislodged stone, broken off from its source. Crouching down on the grass, she examined it before stuffing it inside her sweater's pocket. She stood, wiping her hands dry on her pant. Closing her eyes, she asked, "What have I missed, Jesus?" Common expressions flooded her mind: missed the train, missed the mark, missed the boat, missed diagnosis, missed the point. Her eyes flew open. Missed diagnosis or stated more accurately, misdiagnosis!

Casey intentionally took small steps as she made her way out of the labyrinth, continually praying for enlightenment on what must be Mandy's misdiagnosis. Who would believe her? Certainly not Dr. Alisha. When she stepped out of the labyrinth, she caught sight of a lone figure sitting on the nearby bench. Mandy.

"I was debating whether or not I should return to the centre," Mandy said as Casey drew near, "but I decided to wait. You seemed deep in thought. When you stood at the heart of the labyrinth, so still, it seemed like you were praying. Were you?"

Casey wondered how she should respond while swiping the dew off the bench with her hand. What would a therapist do? It didn't matter, she quickly concluded, as she was here at God's request. She sat down on an angle, facing Mandy. "I was. I prayed for understanding behind a word that came to mind."

"You're a believer?" Mandy asked with reserved excitement while unconsciously fingering the partially hidden necklace under her light jacket. "In what?"

"In Jesus. What about you?"

"Same. I don't like to advertise it as people seem to judge me by it," she replied as she revealed the cross pendant she wore.

"The only judge you need to concern yourself with is Christ," Casey asserted. "If you're right with Him, then that's all that matters."

"In here, I know that," pointing to her heart, "but my mind fights me on it."

"Ask the Holy Spirit to help conform your mind to your heart's desires as you walk the labyrinth. Listen for His truths and guidance."

Mandy pushed herself off the bench. "Will you wait for me?"

"Absolutely," Casey replied, making herself more comfortable on the cold bench. As she watched her client wander the stone-edged path, she thought back to their first meeting, when Mandy had insulted her at the buffet table. She'd progressed significantly since that time. Casey reflected on their counselling sessions. Was Dr. Alisha correct? Had she missed something? Suddenly she was on her feet, having witnessed Mandy's fall, but Mandy had gotten up and waved her off. As she appeared to be okay, Casey returned to the bench. Whatever was missed had to be psychological; God had given her the role of a health psychologist.

As Mandy neared the labyrinth's opening, Casey walked over to meet her. "Any revelations?" she asked.

"Afraid not, as I couldn't focus. I've got a blasted headache again. It appears the doctor needs to re-evaluate my medication as I may be experiencing a side effect - vision loss."

"Your vision? Let's check in on the doctor before we go in for breakfast," suggested Casey trying to retain control of her voice so as not to alarm her. Only Dr. Alisha wasn't in. Casey accompanied Mandy to the living room, insisting she rest on the couch while she rang the doctor from her office.

"What you're recounting isn't related to the medication I prescribed," Dr. Alisha stated from her hands-free car phone. "It may be a migraine, but I doubt it as she hasn't indicated any sensitivity to smells, light, or sound. Unfortunately, the cover-off physician I had arranged to come in had to cancel at the last minute due to a family emergency. As I'm not back until this evening, have the nurse take her to the clinic in town."

Casey agreed to relay the message, only it wasn't in person but by phone, as the nurse was already at the clinic with a client who had fractured an ankle. The nurse instructed Casey to speak with the Director to have a driver assigned. She'd meet Mandy at the clinic.

Before going to find Deborah, Casey checked in on Mandy. She became increasingly concerned when Mandy confided that her vision loss was worsening. "Forget the clinic," Casey said. "I'm taking you to Mountainview Hospital."

"It'll be a waste of time. I've undergone tests there before. They didn't find anything then; I doubt they'll find anything now. It'll likely go away with a bit more rest."

"There's definitely something going on," argued Casey. "We're talking about your eyesight, Mandy!"

"Okay! Okay! I'll go to the hospital," she resignedly agreed.

"Hang tight. I need to update the Director on what's transpired."

Deborah provided Casey with a printed list of Mandy's current medications. "I'd take her, but with Dr. Alisha and the nurse off-site, I need to remain here. I'll call the nurse to let her know not to expect you, update the staff, and I'll reorganize schedules to cover your absence. Keep me apprised of the situation."

Mandy linked her arm in Casey's as she cautiously exited The Centre. Together they walked down the ramp and across the gravel terrain to Casey's car. "I guess I don't have to be concerned with my body image anymore," she said.

"What are you talking about?"

"My eyesight has gotten so poor I can barely see what I'm offended at," she replied with a light laugh. Casey opened the door for Mandy and waited as she slipped into the upholstered bucket seat.

"I can't imagine what you're feeling right now but know that you're not alone. You and I are going to find out the cause behind these symptoms you've been experiencing," Casey said, shutting the passenger side door. Once in the driver's seat, she bantered, "Perhaps it's a good thing you can't see too well as I won't have to worry about my passenger critiquing my driving skills."

"Don't be so sure of that," Mandy quipped back. "My body will know when I'm being jostled about, so you better use those driving skills to your advantage. You wouldn't want me to spread stories about you when I get back."

"Ha!" Casey exclaimed as she maneuvered the car out of the parking lot. "I could retaliate by telling stories about you."

"Doubt it. Patient-client confidentiality."

"Yes, there is that sticking issue," she admitted glancing over at Mandy, who had closed her eyes. "What's your preference? Do you want to talk, listen to music, be alone with your thoughts, or sleep?"

"I may be resting my eyes, but I have no intention of sleeping. Besides, I'm so anxious that I couldn't sleep even if I wanted to. Let's talk. It'll keep my mind occupied."

"Okay. But I'd like to ask some personal questions first if that's alright with you. I want to make sure I haven't missed anything."

"Missed anything?"

"Yes. Sometimes vision loss can be stressed induced; emotional trauma that's resurfaced. Perhaps the therapy sessions have triggered an event that has laid dormant for years."

"Like an assault of some kind," volunteered Mandy.

"Exactly. The only traumatic event you recalled was your father's death. Was there anything else?"

Mandy took her time replying. "Nothing as devastating as losing my eyesight," she said. Casey withdrew a hand from the steering wheel to give a reassuring squeeze to Mandy's clutched ones. "When my father died, I did fall into a state of depression for a while, deeper than what I told you," she confessed. "We were remarkably close; it was hard for me to accept he wouldn't be part of my present or future life. There were so many things I missed about him, including stories about my mother. Through him and my maternal aunts, I came to know her. I learned of her likes and dislikes, her talents and follies, her interests and aspirations."

"And what traits of hers do you have?" Casey inquired.

"To begin with, love of nature. It's why I chose this wellness centre."

"What else?" Casey inquired.

"She was a sky-diving instructor. I'm a stockbroker. Can you figure out the connection?"

Casey tapped her steering wheel in contemplation. "You're both risk-takers?"

"Ooh, you're good," chuckled Mandy.

"What about your father. Was he a risk-taker too?"

"I guess you could say that since he owned his own business. But our commonality was the outdoors. We'd hike the rugged mountain trails or kayak the Canadian rivers, but our times together became less as work dominated more of my life. And then he suddenly died from a pulmonary embolism. Part of my depression was the guilt I harboured for not having spent more time with him because I chose to make work my priority over family. I could have done a better job of balancing the two.

"I took a year off. I was fortunate to have been able to afford such a luxury. You see, my dad's software company had a buy-sell agreement in place, which meant the co-owner was obligated to buy out the partner's interest upon death. My dad set it up that way because he knew I had no desire to take over the business."

Casey slowed the car at the impending crossroad. At the stop sign, she turned onto the paved highway. "A year is a long time. Any suicidal thoughts then or now?"

"I'd be lying to you if I said no. My heart ached at his absence, but I never had a plan of action. They were fleeting thoughts, nothing more than that."

"Who or what brought you out of your grief and back into the workforce?"

"Me!" exclaimed Mandy. "I told myself that I'd spent enough time sulking, and if I didn't smarten up, I'd find myself a hundred pounds overweight and on a psych ward. As it was, I had gained twenty-five pounds. I hired a personal trainer and lost most of the weight by the time I returned to work. I also enrolled in art classes. I wasn't much good at it, but it was fun, and I got to meet some great people. Now tell me, do you still think my vision loss may be trauma-induced?"

Casey reflected on what Mandy had shared. She could recount the story with appropriate emotion, and she wasn't perseverating on events. She seemed to have worked through her grief. "I doubt it," Casey finally replied. "What about your best friend, Amelia. You told me you'd known each other since childhood but that you went your separate ways shortly after your father died. I would have thought she'd have been there for you."

"Well, she wasn't."

Casey briefly took her eyes off the road to look at her passenger, surprised at the bluntness of the reply. The face that stared out the window had hardened. "How come?"

"Because I ended it, that's why! What she did was unforgivable. Amelia knew about my weight and self-image struggles. So, what does she drop off at my doorstep? A box labelled maternity clothes! Can you believe it? She didn't need them anymore and assumed I could use them! The nerve of her!"

Casey shook her head as she tried to make sense of it. "Did you check to see what was in the box?"

"Of course I did! And you know what I did next? I ghosted her. I blocked her as a contact on my phone, and I unfriended her on Facebook."

"You were listening to her voice," Casey said.

"I felt utterly humiliated!"

"You were listening to her voice," Casey repeated. "What was the fear you were confronting?"

They had travelled several kilometres in silence before Mandy spoke again. "I was listening to two voices that spoke as one: Amelia's and mine. The maternity clothes were a reminder that I had failed to lose weight. I no longer loved my body or the person inside it, and I struggled to embrace the new me. The fears that were my constant companions: failure, vulnerability, and rejection. I say 'were' because I've come to realize that these fears have held me back. I've let my outward appearance speak for my heart and soul, but not anymore."

"Where's that leave you and Amelia? Can you forgive her?"

Mandy exhaled a large sigh. "Not yet."

"The words of Franciscan Father Greg Plata come to mind. He said: '"At the heart of Christianity is forgiveness. 'Father forgive them for they know not what they do.' "Forgiveness isn't something we do on our own. It is something we choose to do with God's grace," the Franciscan said.'"[1] A click sound drew Casey's attention. Mandy had found the lever to recline her seat. "How about I change the subject? Tell me about your work as a stockbroker."

"Oh, I'm being interrogated on another matter now," grinned Mandy, her closed eyes creasing at the edges.

"Nope. I'm looking for insider trading," she laughed. "Seriously though, tell me what's involved in your role as I know nothing about stockbrokers or stock markets for that matter." For the remainder of the trip, Mandy provided an abridged explanation of financial markets and trading.

---

[1] The Catholic Post, September 11, 2016, page 7, https://now.dirxion.com/ Catholic_Post/library/Catholic_Post_09_11_2016.pdf

Casey entered the hospital's public parking lot pulling into a vacated stall near the building's entrance. Mandy, arm-in-arm with Casey, was guided inside the hospital to the triage nurse's desk. What followed was a series of frank questions by the nurse. Rather than being told to return to the waiting area, they were immediately escorted to a cubicle inside the emergency room doors. Minutes later, a doctor joined them.

"I'm Dr. Martin," said a tall man, his hair slightly greying at the temples. He, too, had questions, the answers documented onto his tablet. At long last, he left the two alone but not before he explained that he was a Fellow and would need to discuss the case with the supervising doctor.

"And I thought reporters were the leaders in asking probing questions," quipped Mandy. "They take second place to this chap."

Casey withdrew a glossy magazine from the holder on the wall. "I'm only glad you didn't compare him to me," which got a giggled response. As Mandy laid on the bed, an arm shielding her eyes from the fluorescent lights, Casey mulled over her symptoms. Her thoughts were interrupted when the Fellow returned with his supervisor.

"I'm Dr. Jesperson," came the terse introduction. He then launched into his list of questions, starting with the bruising on her body, for which Mandy had no explanation. "Is your diabetes under control?" She nodded. "Have you ever had hormone testing completed?"

"A few months back, at this very hospital," Mandy replied.

The doctor took a few minutes to read the report from his tablet. "The test results came back as normal. I'll request another one to ensure nothing has changed. I'm also ordering an MRI based on your symptoms. I'll return once the results are in." He abruptly exited the room.

"Dr. Jesperson might not have the greatest bedside manner, but you couldn't be in better hands. He's quite thorough," assured Dr. Martin. "I'll see you shortly," was his parting comment.

More waiting – for the lab technician to collect Mandy's blood samples, an orderly to take her for the MRI, the orderly to return her to the cubicle room, and the doctors to return. Casey thought 'shortly' was an inadequate adverb to be used in a place like this.

The doctors at long last stepped into the room. Dr. Jesperson came right to the point. "The MRI confirmed my suspicions. You have Cushing's disease."

"Of course," Casey announced in an astonished tone. "I missed the facial features attributing it to your weight gain, Mandy."

"Are you a physician?" challenged Dr. Jesperson, glaring at this young adult with annoyance.

It was Mandy who replied. "She certainly could be, don't you think?"

"Sorry," Casey meekly replied.

"If I may continue, uninterrupted," turning briefly away from Mandy to give Casey a stern stare. "You have a pituitary gland tumour, which is causing your adrenal glands to produce too much cortisol."

"Is it fatal?" Mandy asked, sitting a little straighter.

"No, it's not," he replied, this time with compassion in his voice. "The hormone, called cortisol, is exceedingly high in your body. We need to get it back within normal limits. We can accomplish this with the surgical removal of the tumour followed by radiation therapy. I'll have you admitted to the hospital today. My Fellow will answer any other questions you may have," and once again, he abruptly left the room.

Casey asked Dr. Martin if the symptoms Mandy had been

experiencing were related to Cushing's disease. She already knew the answer; Mandy didn't.

"The headaches and vision loss? Most definitely. Weight gain also." Dr. Martin's empathy was evident in his kind words to Mandy. "You'll be on the road to recovery in no time. I'm going to speak to the charge nurse to arrange your admission." When the doctor left, Mandy confided her extreme delight in finally knowing the cause to be a physical ailment and not related to anything she was or wasn't doing.

Dr. Jesperson was livid when he read his patient had Cushing's disease. He stormed out of the emergency department in search of Dr. Segan, the endocrinologist who had written up the initial analysis report of Mandy's hormone levels. He found his long-time friend in his office, placing papers into a briefcase. "Blake! I need a few moments before you head home."

Dr. Segan looked up, then set his briefcase on his desk. "What's up?"

"This," Dr. Jesperson said, shoving a paper at him. "You wrote that the test results were negative. I had it redone and found the opposite."

"Really? Leave it with me," insisted Dr. Segan taking the paper with a shaky hand and stuffing it into a desk drawer. "I'll sort it out."

"Blake. You signed off on it. This is on you! And you know I can't just leave it. There have been rumours about your performance of late. I ignored them as I believed them to be just that, rumours. Now, I'm not so sure." Joel looked disheartened at the man who stared blankly back at him. "Look, we've been friends for many years. What's going on? It's not like you to make such blatant errors."

"It won't happen again," Dr. Segan insisted while snatching his briefcase. He appeared to stagger as he made his way to the door.

Dr. Jesperson grabbed his arm. "You know I have to report this! Blake, please, tell me what's going on."

Dr. Segan yanked his arm free. "Nothing is going on! You said you're a friend, so be one!" He disappeared out of the office doorway, leaving Dr. Jesperson standing there in complete puzzlement as to what had just transpired.

Upstairs, on the inpatient unit, Casey was saying her goodbyes to Mandy. She deposited a small stone onto her overhead table. "A token gift for you."

"A piece of stone? Am I supposed to throw it at someone?" Mandy asked flippantly.

"The exact opposite. This piece broke off from one of the stones inside the labyrinth's centre. I want you to hold on to it as you walk the labyrinth in your mind. Take it with you when you stroll the halls of this hospital. Reach for it when you pray words of praise or need. Let it remind you of Christ, the maker of heaven and earth, 'who is, and who was, and who is to come.'" (Rev.1:8 NIV)

Mandy held the stone tightly in her palm. "I will. Thank you."

"And, perhaps, it's time to consider mending a broken relationship with a dose of forgiveness."

She looked at the stone she held in her hand. "Perhaps."

"Goodbye, Mandy. I'll call you as I'm restricted to The Centre's grounds."

"You mean it's too far to drive," she teased.

"Not for you," Casey replied as she scanned the room for her jacket, quickly realizing she'd left it in the emergency department.

"I haven't thanked you for all you've done for me."

Casey took a protracted look at her watch. "I can spare fifteen minutes. Will that be long enough?"

Mandy threw the magazine she'd been holding at her.

"Oh, you!" she facetiously laughed before a solemn expression replaced it. "You are an extraordinary young lady, Casey. I want you to know that. This past week your teachings hit home. I had believed that society's measuring stick didn't influence me, but nothing could be further from the truth. I learned that I'd never love my body until I come to love myself, from the inside out."

"The same way God sees and loves you. He looks at your heart and actions, not the external body."

"I'll try to love myself more deeply, stopping before I reach the narcissist level."

Casey threw the magazine back at her. "Sounds like an attainable goal," she said, smiling widely. A student nurse entered with a blood pressure machine. "Someone else wants your attention. Take care, Mandy. We'll talk soon."

Taking the stairwell down to the main level, Casey silently prayed during the descent: Lord, thank you for having the right people there to diagnose Mandy. Please give her the peace and strength required for her to master the journey ahead. Thank you for identifying the missed-diagnosis.

Casey re-entered the emergency department, slipping through the double glass doors and behind the nurse preoccupied with a patient who spoke broken English. She saw a family vacating the cubicle she and Mandy had been in earlier. Perfect. She beelined it to the room, hoping to reach it before another patient was escorted into it. Inside she found her jacket exactly where she had left it, draped over the back of a plastic stool.

There was a lot of commotion stirring in the room next door. A young patient's voice was escalating, drawing numerous people's attention: staff, patients, visitors. She decided to use this distraction to disappear out of the room and out of the department. She got as far as the nursing station when a flying tissue box hit the counter.

A rattled-looking nurse scurried directly towards the station. She approached the desk, gripping the counter tightly. "The doctor wants a preloaded syringe." She proceeded to name the drug, which Casey knew to be a sedative.

"Then why are you still here?" the nurse tersely asked. "Get him what he needs!" This same nurse nudged her colleague, cocking her head sideways. "Student nurse."

Curiosity had Casey pause longer at the desk than she had intended. She, too, listened in on the room with the action. Dr. Jesperson's authoritative voice could be heard over the general hubbub of the department. "Jeremy. Settle down," he implored. "We're trying to get a history from you to determine how best to treat you."

"You keep asking me what drugs I've been on," the boy screamed. "I'm not an addict."

Dr. Jesperson's voice remained calm but firm. "It's standard procedure. It helps us understand what may be causing you to be sick."

"You're lying!" retorted Jeremy as he tried to storm out of the room. He was a teenager about the same age as Casey's brother, Aaron. Twelve years, possibly younger. When his jacket's sleeve was taken hold of by Dr. Jesperson, the doctor was rewarded with a left hook to the nose sending him flying against a wall, blood visibly flowing. An orderly dashed forward in an attempt to restrain the youth but found himself blocked when Jeremy shoved a cart in his direction. People scattered everywhere as Jeremy frantically tried to find an escape route. Everyone that is but Casey, who sedately walked towards Jeremy, who by this time had barricaded himself behind a couple of chrome-wire shelving units laden with sheets, towels, and other hospital supplies.

Casey held out her hands, palms up, as she unhurriedly approached him. "Jeremy," she called out with kind authority. "My name is Casey, and I'm a visitor here; I'm not hospital staff.

See? I'm wearing street clothes, like you," she said. "I noticed your colourful bracelet and necklace. Who made them for you?"

He watched her through the rack shelves, his eyes darting wildly about.

"Who made it for you?" she repeated in a room that had fallen eerily quiet as all watched the interaction, including Dr. Jesperson, who held a bloodied towel against his face. He had positioned himself behind Casey, the nursing station counter separating them. Casey spotted a couple of security guards approaching noiselessly from Jeremey's blindside. She turned her whole body briefly towards them, effectively blocking Jeremey's view so that she could hand signal for them to back off. Her screwed-up face and tense body relaxed when their advancement stopped. She turned to face Jeremy again. Tapping her finger on her wrist, she tried to get the boy's attention while repeating the question.

Looking at the woven bracelet on his wrist, he replied. "A little girl."

"Where? Here in town or out of the country?"

"In Burkina Faso."

"Ah, you've been to Africa," Casey confirmed as she edged a little closer, remaining in his site line. She'd been there herself as a teenager while on a mission trip. "I bet the girl was delighted you bought it from her."

"Lots of kids were pressuring me to buy their stuff. She just sat on the dirt street, her dark eyes staring up at me as I walked by."

"You connected with your eyes. How lovely. When did you get back?" Jeremy was beginning to pace back and forth. She repeated the question.

"A few days ago," he answered as he randomly pushed items off the shelf.

"And did you get sick on your trip?"

"I'm not on drugs!" he said, kicking hard at a box on the lower shelf.

"I believe you. I do." Casey knew that part of the country to have an abundance of health concerns and a lack of adequate health care. "You might have gotten sick while you were visiting there. Did you?" she asked, moving horizontally with him to maintain eye contact. Jeremy admitted that he had.

"And did you get a stomachache?" asked Dr. Jesperson gently. Hearing the doctor's voice elicited renewed yelling from Jeremy and plastic emesis basins thrown over the racks.

The security guards, who had been waiting at a safe distance, ran nearer, but Dr. Jesperson flung his hands wildly about, bloody towel and all. "Wait just a little longer," he hissed to them. "She's onto something." In an undertone, he requested Casey to ask if he'd experienced any headaches, dizziness, itchy skin, or nightmares.

"Listen to my voice, Jeremy," Casey pleaded while dodging a kidney basin. "Jeremy. Focus on me, on my voice," Casey firmly demanded. She was a few feet away from him. If she could get him to come out from behind the wall of carts, then the staff could do the rest. His eyes seemed wild as they continuously scanned the room. No, not wild. They were full of panic and fear. She called out his name a few more times, and finally, he settled long enough for her to ask about his symptoms.

"What if I did?" Jeremy yelled, shaking the cart with both hands. A rookie police officer flashed his badge at the two security guards then pushed his way through, Taser gun raised. Jeremy saw him. In a fit of anger, he tried to drive one of the carts into the officer's path, but as its wheels were locked, it toppled instead. As Casey scrambled to escape, she heard the Taser gun firing. Simultaneously, items sailed off the top shelf. One heavy box knocked her to the ground, followed by the rack itself. Seconds later, her world went dark.

CHAPTER 5

Chaos ensued in the Emergency department. Dr. Jesperson saw his Fellow dashing towards him because of his bloody nose. "Take care of her!" he insisted, casting concerned eyes briefly upon Casey's motionless body beneath cartons and the shelf. Dr. Jesperson began tossing boxes aside to clear a path to Jeremy. He reached the youth, the officer standing over him with his Taser gun at his side. "Put that thing away!" Dr. Jesperson ordered in a steely voice as he knelt. "And where's that sedative needle I asked for?" he bellowed.

Jeremy laid supine on the cold floor, his eyes staring, unseeing, at the ceiling. The officer holstered his Taser but remained at the scene. "Does he look like someone in need of the likes of you? Stand back, to where I can't see you," came the fierce demand. He called out the boy's name while he flashed a light beam into his eyes to check for reaction and ensure there was no cranial bleeding. He nodded with relief that they showed healthy functioning. Jeremy's eyes soon came into focus.

"I'm Dr. Jesperson. Do you remember me?" The boy nodded, staring at the broken nose. The doctor smiled. "Don't worry about the nose. It'll heal. I bet you're feeling some pain yourself, right?" The boy responded with a weak yes. "And your muscles, do they ache?" The boy again said yes as he rubbed his sore shoulder. The doctor's furrowed brows and pinched mouth conveyed what he thought of the Taser blast outcome. He reached for a couple of towels and tenderly placed them under the boy's head. "I'm going to give you something shortly to ease the pain. Then we're going to help you stand so you can get onto a stretcher. Much more comfortable than being on the floor, wouldn't you agree? You're doing great, Jeremy."

The boy was starting to squirm, agitation beginning again. Not waiting any longer, Dr. Jesperson took the syringe from the nurse's hand and injected it into Jeremy's arm muscle.

"Where's my mom? I want my mom!"

"She should be here any moment. Remember, she was taking your sister to the washroom."

Jeremy's body relaxed. "Oh, ya." There was a brief pause before he spoke again, anxiety in his voice despite the medication in his system. "What's happening to me?"

"Nothing that we can't fix," Dr. Jesperson reassured him. He stood to lock the wheels on the stretcher that had arrived; a nurse helped him get the boy onto it. Having checked off items on a lab requisition form, Dr. Jesperson handed the paper to the nurse requesting stat results, an inpatient room to be secured, and his parent to be brought immediately to him.

When a lab technician came in to draw blood from the drowsy boy, Dr. Jesperson requested a nurse remain while he checked in on Casey. The officer, thankfully, had relocated to the nursing station to write up his report. A security officer was assigned to the boy, the hospital not taking any chances on a possible repeat performance.

Casey had awoken from the incident to find herself lying on

the floor. It took several seconds for her to recollect what had happened. The shelf was upright again, bare of all its contents. She attempted to raise herself onto her elbows.

"Not so fast. You just lay back down," insisted Dr. Martin. "And stay put, at least for a little longer as I requested the head of ER to clear a path for us. It's not every day that I get to tell him what to do." His fingers brushed back her bangs to assess her head wound. A nurse arrived, producing a large, sterile dressing pad, which he taped temporarily over the bleeding cut. "Does it feel like you've broken anything?"

"No, I'm fine."

"Good, but we're going to transfer you onto a stretcher all the same." The nurse automatically left, returning with a stretcher. The two skillfully transferred Casey onto the lowered wheeled bed, readjusting it to full height before rolling it into a nearby room, away from the chaotic activities surrounding them. The nurse disappeared, reappearing moments later, carrying a kit.

"You'll need a few stitches to close that cut," Dr. Martin said as the nurse began cleaning the wound. "First, a local anesthetic to the area before I start showing off my sewing skills." She gripped the sheets, releasing them only when she heard the used syringe drop into a basin. "Ready for the sewing?" She responded by closing her eyes.

Dr. Martin was knotting a stitch when Dr. Jesperson walked in. Aware that someone had entered, Casey opened her eyes, then closed them again. "The boy?" she inquired.

"He'll be fine," Dr. Jesperson assured her as Dr. Martin snipped the suture thread, tossing the needle and scissors into the basin. "I'm waiting for blood test results."

"What do you suspect it to be?" she asked. "You had some idea with that line of symptoms you had me ask."

Dr. Jesperson nodded appreciation of the work done. He

stood with his Fellow at the side of her stretcher. The nurse had left with the suture garbage. "I suspect he's experiencing a reaction to a medication used to treat malaria cases. It's a drug we don't use in Canada as it has some nasty side effects, self-endangering behaviour being one of them. Did you suspect it as well?"

"Absolutely not. I'm no doctor," she stated with a smirk.

"But I heard you could be," he said through a playful smile.

Casey was about to get up when Dr. Martin gently pushed her back down. "Oh no you don't. We're sending you to get an x-ray. You took quite the blow to the head."

"I've got a hard head. Use your healthcare dollars on someone who actually needs the service," she said while making another attempt to get up.

This time it was Dr. Jesperson's hand that lightly pressed down on her shoulder. "No can do as your injury happened on hospital property. Liability issues and such," he said with a wry smile as he raised the side bed rail.

She stared at his distorted nose and the resulting swelling. "It seems you need the x-ray more than I do."

"No need. I know my nose is broken." He bent down to whisper in her ear. "I'm not keen on having it restored to its previous position. I hear it's painful."

Casey gurgled as she closed her eyes against the overhead lights. She relented, knowing she'd not be able to leave the hospital without having the test completed. The men left, leaving her to wait alone for the orderly to arrive. He was a burly fellow with excellent driving skills. He deftly negotiated her stretcher past the nursing station where Dr. Jesperson stood conversing with two police officers, out of the emergency department, and into the radiology and imaging wing.

Casey had eavesdropped on Dr. Jesperson's conversation

with the female police officer and the Taser-happy rookie as her stretcher rolled by them. The doctor was firm with them that they'd have to wait until his patient returned from imaging before he'd grant permission for questioning. Casey was grateful for the reprieve as it allowed her time to recollect all that had happened, from the time she stepped into the next-door cubicle to retrieve her jacket until the present time, waiting for an unnecessary x-ray. Her jacket! She snorted lightly. Abandoned, yet again.

It was quite some time before Casey was able to leave the hospital for the drive back to The Centre. The female police officer had asked her to write out a statement while it remained fresh in her mind. The hospital also needed her to complete paperwork and debrief with one of their occupational health and safety staff. She knew their motive to be a risk assessment for possible legal liability, something she'd never consider as it was an unintentional and unfortunate accident.

Having received permission to leave, Casey went searching for her jacket. The Emergency Department had returned to emergency room normalcy. She spotted her jacket lying in a heap on a gurney. Donning it, she exited through the automatic doors to the fresh outdoors.

In the parking lot, Casey slipped in behind the wheel of her car. She leaned against the steering wheel and talked to God. "Thank you, Jesus, for giving me the courage to approach Jeremy. Don't think I didn't see your hand in all this. You knew I'd recognize Jeremy's hand-made string bracelet and necklace in the colours of the Burkina Faso flag. And I couldn't abandon him when everyone ran the opposite way, not when he reminded me of my younger brother and with eyes full of fear and apprehension. Thank you for helping me keep my wits about me. Thank you for saving two lives today: Mandy's and Jeremy's. You're a good, good father."

Dr. Jesperson was standing at his office window, watching Casey make her way to her car. Dr. Martin joined him. "How's the nose?"

"Painful to touch, but it'll be fine in a few days." They watched Casey get into her car and lean against her steering wheel.

"Hopefully, she will be too," Dr. Martin said.

"She'll recover. She proved herself to be a capable young lady, showing compassion, quiet temperament, and self-control throughout a volatile situation. She's likely exhausted and overwhelmed with all that occurred."

Casey had started her car, reversing it out of the stall. Dr. Jesperson moved away from the window, quickly forgetting about her. He had more pressing matters to contemplate, such as reporting a colleague–friend to the hospital's director. Gingerly, he touched his nose. Tomorrow would be soon enough. Dr. Jesperson laid a hand upon his colleague's shoulder. "I'm calling it a day. See you tomorrow."

The following day, Dr. Jesperson gave a crisp knock on Dr. Sarah Chipsten's office door. He stood before the Director, relaying his concerns and the facts as he knew them. The response he received regarding his colleague's conduct wasn't what he'd expected. Apparently, he hadn't revealed to the Director anything she wasn't already aware of, which raised his ire. "Then what are you going to do about it?" he said, slapping his palms on her desk. "People's lives are at stake!"

Dr. Chipsten eased back into her chair, the realization suddenly dawning on her. "He hasn't told you."

"Told me what?" he asked irritably.

"Please, sit down, Dr. Jesperson. She waited as he took a seat, his wary eyes locked on her. "Dr. Segan is retiring."

"Retiring?" Dr. Jesperson was stunned at this revelation as

his friend never mentioned his intention; neither did the hospital grapevine.

"He submitted his formal resignation last week. I've granted his request for an early departure, waving the requisite notice."

"I don't understand," he said in an almost inaudible voice.

"Only a select few people know. He wanted it that way."

The room was quiet as Dr. Jesperson digested the news, the hospital Director waiting for the questions he was bound to ask. What he said next shocked her. "Is this about his negligence, or is it about the hospital covering their own?"

Dr. Chipsten's jaw tightened. "You've got a lot of nerve to insinuate a hospital conspiracy, Dr. Jesperson!" A few seconds passed before she spoke again. "I can see how you may have reached that conclusion. You can breathe easy as the hospital hasn't been negligent, and apparently, neither has Dr. Segan.

"Dr. Segan has been reviewing all his reports as far back as five months. We're having them double-checked by an impartial endocrinologist. And before you ask, yes he does know, as he was the one who insisted an outside person be brought in. Neither has found any errors to date." Dr. Chipsten acknowledged that she knew about Dr. Jesperson's case. "Here, read this," she said, handing him a typed report. "I found it under my door this morning."

Dr. Jesperson reviewed the document, reading aloud the result. "A false negative." He gave his head a dejected shake. "I don't understand. Why's he resigning when the accusations against him are untrue?"

Dr. Chipsten leaned forward, hands clasped on her desk. "You're asking the wrong person, Joel."

A short time later, Dr. Jesperson rested against the doorjamb of his friend's office, watching as he clicked keys, read the computer screen, and jotted down notes on a pad. The hand tremors were evident.

Dr. Segan absently looked away from the screen, doing a double-take when he realized who stood in his office doorway. "I'm busy, Joel. What do you want?"

Dr. Jesperson gently closed the door. "I've come to offer my apologies. I was out of line. It happens, a trifle more often than it should," he ruefully admitted.

His colleague flicked up his chin. "Is your facial realignment the result of another such trifling event?"

"Hazards of the emergency room," he said, stopping to check his reflection in the office mirror before adjusting his tie. "Still looks pretty bad, doesn't it, even with the make-up?" That got the reaction he was hoping for from his colleague.

Dr. Segan guffawed loudly. "Revlon® or Lancôme®?" Dr. Jesperson turned about, arms crossed, his face posing the question. "Oh, don't give me that look! I know those brands as I'm confronted by them daily, courtesy of my Dorothy and the clutter she leaves on our bathroom counter."

Dr. Jesperson turned back to the mirror, having withdrawn a bottle from his jacket. He unscrewed the lid and dabbed foundation on a particularly purplish spot under his eye. "The young lady behind the cosmetic counter was quite helpful as she taught me the order of things: concealer, foundation, powder. She shared some tips too. I was impressed with the finished results, as were all the lingering women."

"Did you leave your phone number with any of them?"

"You can't be serious. No one would want to go out on a date with someone wearing this face. And definitely not had they learned that a twelve-year-old boy was the amateur boxer that got the best of me." He walked over to a chair, dragging it closer to Dr. Segan. "The Director told me you resigned. Why?"

"Retired," he corrected.

Dr. Jesperson threw up his hands. "Resigned. Retired. Call

it what you want." His tone became sharp as he continued. "You didn't tell anyone; you didn't tell me! Is something wrong with you? With Dorothy? Your kids? Blake, we've been friends for a long time. I want to know!"

Silence ensued as Dr. Segan reached across his desk to pick up the family picture, taken on Qualicum Beach, Vancouver Island, with a glorious sunset backdrop. "Your hypothesis is incorrect," he began as he set the picture back onto its miniature easel. "I'm not experiencing alcohol withdrawal; I haven't touched a drop in over twenty-three years."

Dr. Jesperson's eyes shifted back and forth as he sifted through the symptoms. His head jerked up. "Parkinson's!"

"You forgot the 'plus' word. Parkinson-plus syndrome."

"Oh, no! Which one?"

"Corticobasal Degeneration disease," he said as he stared at the family picture once again. "Source unknown; it's not inherited."

"And it's not curable," added Dr. Jesperson, absorbing the full brunt of the news. His friend's lips tightened as he slowly shook his head. "Then why are you here instead of at home with your family?"

"You're aware that one of the symptoms is cognitive impairment. I began self-doubting myself when a patient's report landed on my desk, querying a possible misdiagnosis. I started reviewing all my files, as I needed to know. I had to be sure I hadn't erred on any of the diagnoses for the sake of the patients and the hospital. Should mistakes be found, the fall-out would be significant. I'm not talking only about hospital lawsuits but the repercussions they would have on Dorothy and the children. I requested a few patients be brought in for retesting."

"And..."

"We had trouble contacting the last person on my list until she unexpectedly arrived under your care yesterday. You completed the final test for me. Mandy was the only false-negative test in the group. I'm sorry for the psychological consequences it likely had on her and the delay in subsequent treatment."

"It's not your fault, Blake."

"I know. Still, it's unfortunate all the same. As for the other patients' tests, their results supported the original diagnosis, which means the hospital and I are in the clear." He logged out of his computer programs, then powered it down. "My last day is tomorrow."

"Tomorrow! Then what?"

"We'll continue praying for miraculous healing. I know you're not a believer, but Dorothy and I are. I've accepted my diagnosis and prognosis. Grieving is the painful part, the losses as my body and mind become increasingly disabled, along with the many things I can't be a part of or will ever be a part of. Acceptance is such a loaded word, but God-willing, I'll achieve it.

"Dorothy and I are moving to the southern part of the province to be closer to our children and her siblings. I want her to have as much support around her as possible as the next five to eight years will be extremely hard on her, on everyone.

"I've been in touch with the senior neurologist at the Movement Disorder Clinic. He's emailed me various clinical studies being done worldwide, completed ones and those in the recruitment phase. There's one particular study that I'm considering joining.

"Joel, I wanted to tell you so many, many times. I just couldn't bring myself to do it; never the right time and all. Then yesterday morning, Dorothy insisted I tell you, threatening to come by the hospital if I didn't. She would, you know." Dr. Jesperson readily agreed. "I decided to wait until the end of your shift to invite you out for dinner. You ruined everything with your unexpected visit. I was enraged by the assumption you made when I wobbled to the door. Your body language spoke your thoughts. When I heatedly told Dorothy about our encounter, she pointed out that it was a logical conclusion to make. She always could see the bigger picture. I was going to call you today and have you come to my office so that I could explain. He rose unsteadily from his chair. "I haven't given up fighting, not by a long shot. And I sure hope I don't have to resort to cosmetics to enhance my skin colour," he joked weakly.

Dr. Jesperson came around the desk, and the two embraced, each struggling to hold back tears. There were no treatment suggestions he could offer to reverse the irreversible. And there were no words to convey the depth of his sorrow.

Dr. Segan released his hold, drawing tissues from his pocket to wipe his eyes and blow his nose. "Now that you know, Joel, please drop by the house. Dorothy and I would love for you to visit. We're here for another few weeks." Joel promised he would.

CHAPTER 6

At The Centre, Casey was bombarded with questions the moment she stepped inside. The bandage on her forehead and no Mandy following in her wake, being tell-tale signs that much was amiss. Deborah drew her into her office. Dr. Alisha arrived shortly after. Casey relayed all that had happened and assured them that she could finish out her week. It was another hour before she was able to cuddle under her down-filled duvet, to fall instantly asleep the moment her head touched the pillow.

The morning began by reciting a shorter version of yesterday's event to staff and an even slimmer version during morning and afternoon group sessions. Mandy requested her proposed treatment plan be shared with the group, citing that one can't make true friends when secrets are kept.

The final week was as intense as the first one, the difference being that the women were readily engaged. Mandy's illness catapulted them into analyzing more deeply internal and external influences in their lives, which helped align their personal values compass.

As the facilitator, Casey kept the conversations on-topic,

ensuring everyone had an opportunity to speak. And through it all, she challenged them to identify cause and effect, confronted them on what they believed were effective coping strategies, and steered them towards realistic self-care goals. She could see the progress each was making to greater self-awareness. The actual test would be in the real world, outside the bubble The Wellness Retreat Centre offered.

On the last day, Casey presented the women with the same gift she had given Mandy - a small stone. She had thought of the idea as she drove out of the hospital's parking lot, which forced her to make a pit stop at a wedding store to pick up a supply of small organza drawstring gift bags. After one of her early morning prayer times at Lookout Point, she had sifted through the stone pile remnants to gather the treasured pieces. She carried them back to her room, where she scrubbed them clean before praying over the lot. "Lord, bless the possessor of these stones. May each come to know how wonderfully created they are and how rich they are in your abiding grace."

She placed each stone into a gift bag along with a printed note: You are altogether beautiful. It was a partial bible verse from the Song of Solomon, 4:7 (NIV). She didn't reference the scripture verse as it would be against The Centre's policy. Those who knew the bible verse would recognize it. Those that didn't, well, she sincerely hoped they'd come across the quotation in The Book one day.

Casey made a final trip to Lookout Point to spend time in prayer. Before she prayed, she reflected on yesterday's telephone conversation with Mandy. They'd spoken every night since she'd been hospitalized. She learned that Ethan, Dr. Ethan Martin, was also a British native. He visited her daily after his shift ended. They'd found they had more in common besides their homeland. When she texted to say she had something important to share that evening, she assumed it had to do with him. Casey leaned against the gabion wall staring unseeingly at the view before her as the memories of last night's conversation flooded back.

"I did something I thought I'd never do," Mandy began in a voice bubbling over with joy. "I reached out to Amelia, and she's here, sitting at my bedside! Can you believe it? There's been lots of crying, hugging and apologizing. I have Father Plata and you to thank. Father Plata, for those powerful and humbling words. You, for our discussions on the topic of forgiveness. If there was to be any hope of salvaging my relationship with Amelia, I knew I couldn't waste any more precious time on negative thoughts and emotions. I had to surrender," Mandy confessed. "And I chose to do it with God's grace."

Casey's eyes moistened. "That took real courage. You faced possible rejection yet proceeded anyway. I'm proud of you!"

"And that maternity box? It never contained clothes with stretch belly panels or extra fabric flowing from the bust down. Amelia said she had enclosed long-fitting shirts, soft knits, pants with an elastic waistband, and other appropriate apparel. My mistake was reading the brand label, names I knew to be well-known maternity clothes companies. Had I taken a closer look, I would have realized that I could have worn those items. The word *maternity* on the box blinded me, as did the labels. I was judge and jury, convicting Amelia without giving her a chance to defend herself."

Amelia spoke over Mandy's voice. "I've been pardoned," she laughed.

"We're on good terms again," Mandy confirmed. "We're clasping hands as I speak."

Casey didn't need to be present to attest that her gemstone client was shining from the inside-out. Mission accomplished.

The morning breeze carried the fresh smell of conifer trees

and brought Casey back to the present. "Your creation surrounds me," she said, stretching her arms out in praise. It brought to mind the 10,000 Reasons (Bless the Lord) song, co-written by Matt Redman and Jonas Myrin. She sang it aloud over the valley and hummed the tune all the way back to The Centre.

By mid-morning, the front entrance had swelled with women gathered to convey parting well-wishes. It was heartwarming to watch them exchange phone numbers and addresses and make promises to stay in touch. Casey was mingling among them, her hand continually dipping into the bag she carried as she handed out her parting gifts. In return, she received hugs and touching appreciative words.

Patricia took her aside to have a private conversation. "I thought you to be a young whippersnapper," she confessed. "I misjudged you, and for that, I must apologize." Casey could feel the blush travel up her neck to her face. "You put me in my place, and rightly so," she said while embracing her. "Thank you, my dear, for opening my eyes."

After the clients had departed, the Director held a staff debriefing. She thanked Casey for covering the vacated position on such short notice and for the labyrinth idea. She went on to remind staff to complete any outstanding progress notes. Casey tuned her out when she spoke about program changes and which staff members would be on holiday when the next group of ladies arrived. When the meeting ended, Deborah shook hands with Casey, offering her platitudes. The others did likewise, except for Teresa, who suggested they visit the labyrinth one last time.

Casey strolled over the freshly cut lawn alongside Teresa. "And you thought I was crazy when I raised the labyrinth idea." Her companion was quick to point out that she wasn't the only one who thought it; most everyone did.

"There were moments when I doubted we could pull it

off," Teresa admitted, "especially when the women began to balk at completing phase two. But in the end, a little friendly competition was all it took to unite the women."

Casey punched the air with a one-two combination. "Boxing Divas and Her-ricanes. They got into it, didn't they?"

"They sure did. And yesterday, when I was standing before the second-floor window, do you know who I saw stepping into it? Take a guess."

Casey shook her head as they started on their return walk. "I've no idea. Deborah perhaps?"

"Close. Dr. Alisha!"

"Then we can presume she won't be dismantling it, although she'll probably replace the natural grass path once it gets trodden down to dirt level. Likely flagstones or some similar type of landscaping product to keep it aesthetically pleasing," ventured Casey.

"Perhaps I should suggest gravel. I could get the next group of women to wheelbarrow it in from the driveway."

Casey laughed. "She strikes me more as the synthetic turf type. No water or mowing required."

They had reached Teresa's vehicle, where the two embraced in friendship. "I'm going to miss you."

"For you," Casey said as she handed over the last gift bag. "A keepsake from our labyrinth experiment." They hugged once more before parting ways. As Casey waved a final goodbye, she thought of how Teresa's personality manifested her heart.

Mandy had received phone calls from various ladies at The Centre once her situation had been broadcasted. A few dropped in after their release/parole/discharge; terms humorously used to describe their two-week stay. She was dumbfounded when Patricia entered her hospital room.

Pink Lady had crossed a critical threshold when she decided

she'd be the sole judge of her appearance and choice of friends. Society had finally lost its grip on her. Old money and new money had found common ground, and it looked as if a friendship was blossoming as a result.

Casey was on the four-lane highway, having changed lanes to pass a semi-trailer, when her cell phone rang. She glanced at the Caller ID before pressing the accept button on her infotainment display. "Hi Dad. Just so you know, I'm driving."

"I understand; I'll keep it short. We won't be home this afternoon as the boys and I decided to check out a farm auction. Don't worry about dinner. We'll pick up pizza."

"Sounds good. See you later." She disconnected the call and switched her radio station to something more uptempo. She had a few hours of highway driving ahead of her.

At long last, Casey turned onto Rocky Meadows' driveway. She parked near the front of the house and had barely opened her door when Harley, their Blue-Heeler dog, stuck his head in and began nuzzling his snout into her hand. "Hi there, boy. Did you miss me?" she asked, rubbing his head ruffly with both hands. "Yeah, I missed you too."

She retrieved her suitcase and jacket from the trunk. Repositioning the purse strap on her shoulder, she draped the jacket over her forearm and raised the telescopic luggage handle. With Harley bouncing at her side, she made her way to the house. "Sorry, Harley. You know you can't come in," she said, gently pushing him back so she could close the door. She peeped through the door window to see if he was still there. He wasn't. He was dashing toward the cow pen. "Your feelings don't stay hurt for long," she said as she hung up her jacket and kicked off her shoes. She dropped her purse beside her suitcase. "I could do with a cup of tea," she said on a yawn.

Carefully, she carried her hot cup of mint tea to the living room, placing it on an end table. She dropped in the upholstered chair, stretching out her legs. What an incredible couple of weeks, she thought. She knew the counselling skills God had given her were gone but couldn't pinpoint exactly when they had left her. She no longer knew things like the history of labyrinths or the symptoms associated with Cushing's disease.

Reaching over for the guitar that leaned against the wall, Casey laid the lower bout on her lap, positioning her fingers over the neck's strings. She strummed a few chords of Beautiful, by MercyMe. Before long, she was singing through all the verses. She sang it for women everywhere. While singing the chorus, she was interrupted by the muffled ringing from her cell phone. It was playing the business ringtone! Scrambling out of her chair, she raced to her purse, fumbling to reach it in time. "Kallan Temporary Staffing Solutions," she answered, with laboured breathing.

"Hi. I'm calling from Blue Pots Restaurant. We require a waiter or waitress to start this coming weekend. Is that a position your agency offers?"

Casey envisioned working in an elegant establishment. "Yes, it is," she replied as she quickly walked to her father's office to grab paper and a pen. Her vision was short-lived when she learned she was to work at a fast-food place. She almost laughed aloud with the realization that she'd been a health psychologist at a prestigious wellness centre only two hours ago. What issues will my new gemstone client be confronting, she wondered while writing down her next assignment's address.

GROUP DISCUSSION QUESTIONS

1. Take-out exercise. Casey had asked her group to "identify two objects you would take out of your home if it were engulfed in flames. It can't be photos. And it can't be alive, like a person or a pet." What would you take out? Share with your group why you chose those objects.

2. The women in the story regretted not having the body they once had or always wanted. Name the regrets you carry. Share them with the group. If you feel uncomfortable sharing, write them down for personal reflection.

3. Read 1 Peter 5:8. What is the meaning behind the warning if you were to apply it to regrets?

4. What are some ways Satan manipulates our feelings?

5. Casey said: "They're completing their exercise routines, eating healthy, and understanding the concepts of lifestyle

change, but it's not enough because what they're doing is action without heart." Teresa rephrased it by saying they lacked a committed spirit. What does having a committed spirit look like?

6. Read Proverbs 16:3. How will our thoughts be established?

7. Read Romans 12:1-2. What does the apostle Paul ask of us?

8. A labyrinth is not a maze with a dead-end but a circuit path leading one to walk to its centre and then return the same way out. What are the benefits of walking a labyrinth?

9. A labyrinth should never become a ritual, nor the only method of praying. It is merely a tool that helps us silence our active minds so that we can attentively pray and listen. What are the dangers of making a labyrinth your prayer ritual?

10. Where are your quiet places to pray and listen?

11. Read together Philippians 4: 6-9 (NIV): Do not be anxious about anything, but in every situation, by prayer and petition, with thanksgiving, present your requests to God. And the peace of God, which transcends all understanding, will guard

your hearts and your minds in Christ Jesus. Finally, brothers and sisters, whatever is true, whatever is noble, whatever is right, whatever is pure, whatever is lovely, whatever is admirable - if anything is excellent or praiseworthy—think about such things. Whatever you have learned or received or heard from me, or seen in me - put it into practice. And the God of peace will be with you.

Prayer Time Direction
Adoration: Praise God, our creator and redeemer.
Confession: Be truthful with your struggles.
Thanksgiving: Give thanks for available support, resources, and answered prayers.
Supplication: Pray for your needs and the needs of others.

Printed in the United States
by Baker & Taylor Publisher Services